# WORLD'S END

# The Phoenix Rising Trilogy

*Elissa's Quest*
*Elissa's Odyssey*
*World's End*

PHOENIX RISING

III

# WORLD'S END

ERICA VERRILLO

Random House New York

Text copyright © 2009 by Erica Verrillo

Jacket illustration and frontispiece map copyright © 2009 by Omar Rayyan

Published in the United States by Random House Children's Books, a division of Random House, Inc., New York.

Random House and the colophon are registered trademarks of Random House, Inc.

Visit us on the Web! www.randomhouse.com/kids

Educators and librarians, for a variety of teaching tools, visit us at www.randomhouse.com/teachers

*Library of Congress Cataloging-in-Publication Data*
Verrillo, Erica F.
World's End / by Erica Verrillo. — 1st ed.
p. cm. — (Phoenix rising trilogy ; [bk.] 3)
Summary: Still not accustomed to her life as a princess, Elissa, learning on the eve of her fifteenth birthday that she is to be bethrothed to a man of her father's choosing, runs away and, after many difficulties, reunites with her friends to finally fulfill the prophecy of the Phoenix.
ISBN 978-0-375-83950-4 (trade) — ISBN 978-0-375-93950-1 (lib. bdg.) —
ISBN 978-0-375-83951-1 (pbk.) — ISBN 978-0-375-85389-0 (e-book)
[1. Magic—Fiction. 2. Human-animal communication—Fiction. 3. Healers—Fiction.
4. Fantasy.] I. Title.
PZ7.V61315Wo 2009
[Fic]—dc22
2008019280

Printed in the United States of America

10 9 8 7 6 5 4 3 2 1

First Edition

For my daughter, Maya

# Contents

WESTERN REACH

NORTHERN

Leonne

Citadel of the Khan

High
Steppes

Wilderness

Great Oasis

SOUTHERN DESERT

Alhamazar

Elissa's
World

# WORLD'S END

# Prologue

The Ancient One stood gazing at her hearth. The fire was out, as it had been for quite some time, its embers now cooled to lifeless gray ash. She was perched on one leg, her chin tucked deeply into the cowl of her dark robe. The Ancient One had no idea how long she had been standing in that awkward pose, nor did she care. Her interest in such insignificant matters had long since died.

The Ancient One snorted in disgust.

"If you want something done right, you just have to do it yourself," she muttered. "I'll have to put my foot down before that scatterbrained child gets completely off track."

Slowly, stiffly, the Ancient One lowered her foot.

"The longest journey . . . ," she began.

She paused and looked about the darkened room, mentally calculating the time it would take to reach her destination; counting the weeks, days, and hours it would require to draw the Seeker there—and the Others as well.

". . . begins with a single step."

Without sparing a glance for the hearth, the three-legged stool tossed carelessly on its side, the crooked stick, or the room that had been her home for eons, the Ancient One passed through the doorway, and, with a great gust of wind and a fierce flapping of her robes, she cast herself into the world.

# ✤ 1 ✤

---

# The Castle by the Sea

Castlemar, the Castle-by-the-Sea, stood on a high bluff overlooking the great expanse of rough gray water for which it had been named. From a distance, the castle looked like a giant's crown, its battlements, turrets, and towers rising above an impassive limestone face. Unlike the cliff it rested on, the castle walls were made of durable granite, so hard that the perpetual sea winds could not erode them. Originally the stone had been polished to such a high sheen that the central tower reflected the morning sun like a beacon, but decades of salt-laden breezes had roughened its exterior so that now the stone gleamed only in the cracks and crevices that had escaped the aging effects of the wind.

The granite had been hauled from the northern mountains so long ago that nobody could remember who had ordered such a huge undertaking, but it must have been someone with a large labor force at his disposal, a navy, and many enemies, for the castle walls were impregnable. The battlements commanded an admiral's view of the limitless waves. But on clear days, such as those that arrive after a storm, the view from the top of the castle's principal tower rivaled that of an eagle, for from there one could see the snow-capped peaks of the mountains of the Great Circle, beyond which there was nothing but sky.

On this clear, bright morning, Princess Elissa of Castlemar was making her way slowly down the upper hallway to the stairs that led from the royal apartments to the main hall. She was dressed in her finest brocade gown and her most elaborate lace collar in order to present herself to the King. For although the King was her father, court etiquette demanded that she pay him due respect in both dress and manner. In private she might call him "Father" and he might even pat her on the head, but in public he was always "my lord."

Elissa approached the staircase with caution, for the heels of her shoes were elevated and she had not had sufficient practice walking in them. Before coming to Castlemar as its Princess and sole heir, she had worn the simple full skirts and blouse of a peasant. For that was how she had been raised. And in spite of all the tutoring and training she had received while at Castlemar, she was still a country girl at heart. The stiff gowns and even stiffer manners of Court appealed to her not in the least, and the restrictions imposed upon her by her shoes were almost unbearable. She surveyed the curving length of the stairs before her and contemplated her mission, which was to descend without suffering the embarrassment—and pain—of broken bones. Elissa positioned herself so that when she grasped her uncooperative skirts in both hands, she could use the inner wall for support by lightly grazing it with her right elbow as she descended. She realized this ploy might be considered cheating, but until she gained the ability to walk blindfolded down a winding, uneven stone staircase on stilts, her dignity would have to be compromised. Of course, if no one actually observed her bumping and tottering down the stairs, her pride might, for once, remain intact.

Unfortunately, Elissa no longer possessed the kind of invisibility required to escape the notice of her peers. It seemed that every time she stumbled, someone was there to see her. This was also the case in every instance in which she used the wrong utensil at dinner, addressed a noble by the wrong title, or thanked a servant. Each time she erred, she was tactfully guided into the proper behavior by her tutors. Still, she knew that no matter how gently her tutors treated her, they, like everyone else, were secretly laughing. She'd like to believe that she was being overly sensitive, as her father insisted, but she knew that her perceptions were accurate. The whispers and giggles that followed in her wake were proof that her title was not taken seriously by anyone *except* her father, who seemed to be oblivious to her cool reception at Court.

Now that she was finally a resident of the castle, Elissa wasn't sure what she had been expecting. Before coming to Castlemar, she had envisioned it as a larger version of Bruno's Manor—a big stone-and-timber house set in a meadow. Since her father was King and Bruno was only the lord of a small holding, she had imagined that perhaps the castle would have more rooms, a larger kitchen hearth, and a fancy dining hall with colored windows. Nothing in her experience could have prepared her for scores of rooms—every one of which boasted its own broad hearth—turrets, towers, and catwalks, with courtyards on every side, barracks, rows of stables, a library, and huge ballroom. And the gardens! There were herb gardens, flower gardens, vegetable gardens, sculpture gardens. There were deer parks, peacock parks, pheasant parks, and meadows for cows, horses, and bees; vineyards, orchards, woodlands, ponds, dovecotes, and kennels. In the ten months that she had been living in the castle, she hadn't covered even a fraction of its grounds.

Elissa was almost giddy with relief. She was nearing the bottom of the staircase and she wasn't dead yet! Her joy, unfortunately, was cut short by the sight of her three lovely, and thoroughly despicable, cousins: Rayna, Vanna, and Lavinia.

It seemed that every noble in Castlemar possessed the same straight dark hair, pale skin, and arrogant bearing. Especially these three, who, while cousins of hers, were somehow not directly related to one another. Elissa wasn't sure how that worked, but her father assured her that such was indeed the case, all appearances to the contrary. To her untutored eyes, the Cousins resembled identical porcelain dolls, all cast from the same delicate mold.

*They're like a bevy of swans,* thought Elissa, looking down at their slender bent necks. *Graceful but nasty.* Whenever she stood beside the Cousins, Elissa felt like an ox. Now all three were halted at the base of the staircase, gazing at her expectantly from canted eyes. No doubt they were waiting for her to fall. Watching Elissa for blunders was one of their most rewarding forms of entertainment.

For once, Elissa managed to shortchange the Cousins of their morning's fun by reaching the bottom step alive and in one piece, her dress still on and her hair almost in place—somehow one small strand of russet hair had worked its way loose from under her golden hairnet. The three girls inclined their shining, elaborately braided heads before her in a token gesture of respect. Their hair had been dressed in a fashionable style that Elissa's lady's maid had given up on after a few fruitless, and painful, skirmishes with Elissa's unruly curls. The hairnet was a second-best choice—better than letting her hair hang loose over her shoulders, which would have been Elissa's preference, but one not quite befitting a princess.

As she passed the three girls, poised gracefully in their deep curtsies, Elissa attempted to shove the stray lock into place. The girls said nothing, of course, nor did they rise, but Elissa could hear a tiny intake of breath and Rayna's almost imperceptible whisper—"Probably on her way to the kitchen"—followed by the inevitable snicker. Elissa continued down the hall, ignoring them, and their giggles, with as much dignity as she could muster.

The Cousins also giggled whenever Favian passed, but for an entirely different reason. They loved his courtly flourishes, his elegant manners, his intriguing foreign accent, and his flattery. Certainly, with his dark, flashing eyes and black hair, he resembled a Castlemar noble much more than she did. If not for his height and the hue of his skin, Favian could easily have passed for one of them. Elissa crumpled her skirt tightly in her fists. She had hoped for something more from him.

Or perhaps just something *else*.

Elissa was brought up short by the faint smell of frying. In her distraction, she had missed the corridor that led to the audience chamber and had walked toward the wing that housed the kitchen.

Elissa looked around to make sure nobody had noticed her. Then she turned, as if she had merely changed her mind, and retraced her steps. *The Cousins were right*, she thought bitterly. *I naturally gravitate toward kitchens.*

The audience chamber, as Elissa recalled, was down the corridor and to the right, through a set of rather imposing paneled doors. Since her arrival, she had been through those doors only once—the night her father had presented her to his court. Elissa had been so nervous that evening, she could hardly recall a moment of it. All she remembered was that her father had held her hand, and that she had kept quiet and still while he placed the golden circlet upon her head.

Fortunately, she had not been required to say anything.

As Elissa turned into the hallway that led to the audience chamber, she felt almost as nervous as she had on her presentation night. Rarely did she see her father by day, though she dined with him every evening. During working hours, her father was King. The fact that he had requested to see her this morning meant that he wanted to speak to her as a king, rather than as a father. Although sometimes she wasn't sure that there was much of a difference.

As she approached the large double doors, the two guards flanking the doorway stood at attention and uncrossed their staffs. The doors swung open and Elissa took a tentative step forward to face the King of Castlemar.

Falk was standing at the far end of the room, waiting to greet her. "Elissa," he called. "Come in."

Cautiously, Elissa made her way across the room. When she reached Falk, she curtsied. "My lord," she murmured. Then she stood and faced her father.

11

Falk greeted Elissa with a warm smile, but there was something in his dark eyes that she could not read, which made her heart falter. All the nobles at Court seemed to share Falk's ability to conceal his true thoughts. It was a skill that Elissa believed she would never be able to master.

"Sit with me," said the monarch. Taking Elissa by the elbow, he steered her to the seats normally reserved for the King's advisors. Elissa sat down heavily upon a cushioned chair and, surreptitiously easing her heels out of her shoes, let out a profound sigh of relief.

"Are you well?" asked Falk sharply. His brow was furrowed in concern.

Elissa nodded. Her father always inquired after her well-being, though she was never anything short of robust.

"I'm feeling just fine," she said.

Falk appeared satisfied with her answer. "Good," he said. There was a silence. "You have grown," he observed.

This much was true. Elissa was a full inch taller than when Falk had first seen her walking across Bruno's Great Hall, hesitantly closing the distance between them. Now, when they faced one another, she could look him directly in the eye. And she was filling out. When Falk looked at her, he could see the promise of future generations. He cleared his throat.

"Elissa," Falk began. "You are going to be fifteen this spring, are you not?"

"Yes," she replied. Her birthday was only a few weeks away. It was hard for her to imagine that two springs ago, she had been plucking herbs for Nana and sleeping in the attic of a simple one-room cottage. Elissa couldn't help but wonder how Nana was faring in her absence. Perhaps she'd found another young apprentice to fetch things for her. For some reason, the thought saddened her.

"In Castlemar it is customary to throw a party when a young woman reaches fifteen years of age," Falk was saying. "In your case, of course, we would hold a court ball and invite the nobility from other kingdoms."

Elissa felt flustered. A ball, for her?

"Will I have to dance?" she asked. If she had to prance about in these shoes, she'd probably never see her sixteenth year.

Falk laughed, disarmed. "Yes, of course, that's

13

the whole point. But don't worry. You will be well instructed by the Dance Master. And the girls will help you."

By "the girls," Falk meant the Cousins. Elissa frowned slightly. She did not wish to offend her father, who at this moment was planning a social event solely for her benefit. But the thought of those simpering faces sneering at her as she stumbled her way across the floor on stilts was more than she could bear.

"That won't be necessary," said Elissa, her voice taut. "The Dance Master will be sufficient."

Falk, to his credit, did not push the matter. After all, the girls were his cousins, too, and he knew them well. It could not have escaped their notice that, unlike Castlemar's nobility, who were small-boned and dark, Elissa was tall and fair— as were a great majority of the servants.

"I can't say that I blame you. The girls can be rather nasty," Falk mused. "Rayna, especially. That child needs a good paddling. I'd do it myself if I wasn't so terrified of her mother."

Elissa's face broke into a broad grin. Rayna's mother, the Duchess of Gaunt, was widely regarded as a harpy. When she visited, novice courtiers stayed at home rather than suffer the sting of her barbed comments, for she always picked on those who were new at Court. Even the guards were afraid of her.

Elissa's smile faded.

"I can see you have reservations," said Falk. "Tell me."

"Well," Elissa began. "I am a little nervous about something."

"What is it?" Falk had anticipated Elissa's concerns about meeting new people, particularly young men, and was prepared to reassure her.

"It's my shoes. I am afraid I will fall down."

"Shoes?" Falk was completely taken aback. He glanced down to where Elissa had raised up her skirts to reveal her high heels. Falk laughed, entirely too hard and for too long.

"Oh my," he gasped. "Young ladies don't dance in those. They wear special slippers for dancing."

Elissa felt tremendously relieved, both at the news and at her father's good spirits. "There is one more thing," she said, emboldened. "Can my friends come?"

Falk hesitated. "Your traveling companions

are, to say the least, highly unusual," he said finally. "However, I think an invitation could be arranged. But are you sure they would *want* to come? After all, Maya is but a child, and Aesha is . . ." Falk did not know how to continue with any degree of tact. Aesha, towering a full head or more over them all and with her white hair and face, looked and acted like a ghost. She was rarely seen outside the confines of her quarters, though the guards sometimes observed her pacing the high parapets on windy days.

Falk's lapse into silence roused a sudden anxiety in Elissa. She knew her father did not approve of her friends. He placed so much value on title. In that respect, he and Favian were very much alike. But how could she make her father accept her companions if he couldn't even see them for who they were?

"You need to begin talking to people of comparable rank and station," Falk said finally.

"What do you mean?" asked Elissa, nonplussed. As far as she was concerned, "people of comparable rank and station" included practically everybody.

"You are a young woman now." Falk spoke

16

slowly, as if explaining something painfully obvious to an uncomprehending child. "The ball will provide an excellent opportunity for you to choose."

"To choose what?"

"To choose your future husband, of course," said Falk. "That's what the coming-out ball is for." Falk leaned forward and patted Elissa's shoulder, somewhat awkwardly. "Rest assured. As a princess—and my daughter—you will be approached only by the finest of Castlemar's nobility."

For a moment or two Elissa sat in her chair, stunned by the turn the conversation had taken. "But . . . but I am only fourteen," she finally stammered. She looked down at her hands, demurely folded in her lap, as if they could enlighten her.

"Soon to be *fif*teen," her father pointed out. "Although you arrived in Castlemar nearly a year ago, you still know very few people, which is, of course, why I have decided to hold a ball for you. There will be many eligible young nobles at the ball. There will also be quite a few older, established lords with holdings and power, and in need of heirs."

Falk pressed his palms together, warming to his argument. "Fifteen is not too young for a union to be arranged," he explained. "Though naturally, one does not need to marry right away. Long engagements, sometimes lasting several years, are generally the rule between young people."

The reason for long betrothals was that the prospective groom might get killed proving himself on the battlefield, or in a duel, before the wedding. Wise parents frequently opted to delay the happy day until they were sure of the groom's ability to defend himself. But Falk decided not to mention this. He tapped his chin thoughtfully. "A more mature man might want to marry sooner, of course. In a matter of months, perhaps."

"*Months?*" Elissa's shock was palpable. "You can't really expect . . ." She jerked her head up as a sudden sharp suspicion hit her. "Is there someone in particular you have in mind?" she asked in a quiet voice.

Falk drew in his breath. "There is," he said cautiously. "My cousin Gavin, the Duke of Cardys, is looking for a bride, now that his wife has passed away."

Elissa's eyebrows drew down into a tight *V.* "Isn't he one of the men who tried to overthrow you?" she asked.

"Why, yes," replied Falk, pleased. "You have an excellent memory. I am sure you'll be able to identify all the lords of the Eastern Reach in no time! Of course, Gavin's lands are not quite as extensive as those of some of my other cousins, but they are very productive. He's a powerful man. And of course there is no better way to secure a lasting alliance than through marriage."

Elissa could not believe what she was hearing. Hadn't Falk traded her for troops to fight this very man? And now Falk wanted her to marry him!

Falk waited for Elissa to reply, allowing her sufficient time to fully grasp the reasonableness of his proposal. And to accept it.

"You are using me again," she said finally, her voice trembling. "I will not marry simply to help you consolidate your power."

"What?" Falk was flabbergasted. "Of course you will! You are a member of the royal family! And political alliances are the sole reason for *all* of our marriages!" He leveled his dark eyes at Elissa, piercing her with his gaze. "You are not a humble peasant girl who marries a boy because of his strong back . . . or because he owns a sword. You are the Princess of Castlemar—and I am its King. You will do as I tell you!"

"Would you have me obey you blindly?" countered Elissa. Her nostrils were flared wide. "Am I your servant? Is that what I must be, in order to be a good . . . princess?" She had meant to say "daughter" but somehow the word got stuck in her throat.

Falk rubbed his eyes in frustration. He had merely intended to give Elissa fatherly direction and guidance, not a set of orders. After everything Elissa had endured at his hands, he had no wish to become her enemy again. "No, no," he said wearily. "You simply need to be sensible."

Elissa rose swiftly to her feet. "I am *already* sensible," she retorted. She kicked off her shoes, knocking them in Falk's direction. "Those," she said, pointing scornfully at the offending footwear, "are ridiculous."

Then, without waiting for Falk's permission

to leave, she hoisted up her skirts and sailed across the chamber. With her head held high, she passed through the two wide doors of the audience chamber like a ship departing for the open seas.

# ∼ 2 ∼

# Oak's Cottage

Elissa paced her chambers, stiff with outrage, her thoughts tumbling like rocks in a landslide. Falk actually intended to force her into marriage! How could he do this to his own flesh and blood? Had he no loyalty? No respect? Elissa dared not even think the word "love." She was too deeply angered by Falk's disregard to admit the true source of her pain: disappointment. Falk had seemed so kind in Gravesport—so fatherly—and now . . . now it seemed he had forgotten all his promises to her. Elissa's head was aching. She needed to talk to a friend—someone who would be sympathetic. But not in this dress. The bulky skirts and long, dangling sleeves of formal court attire were almost as foolish as those silly shoes.

Elissa removed the gown she was wearing,

which was no small accomplishment. Normally it took two maids to get her in and out of her gowns. But Elissa had no desire to summon the servants, so she undid the hundreds of hooks and buttons herself. Then, carefully removing her arms from the sleeves, she slowly slid to the floor and crawled out from under her gown. The dress was still standing.

*Amazing,* she said to herself. *Except for the lack of a head, it could easily pass for me.* It occurred to her that maybe all the other dresses walking around at Court were empty as well, and nobody realized it.

Elissa removed her undergarments until she was down to her shift. Then she turned to the task of finding something else to wear. Elissa breathed a small sigh as she rummaged through her armoire. There was nearly nothing in it. Most of her court clothing was stored in a special room designed just for that purpose, a room she did not have easy access to—unless she wanted to run down the halls in nothing but her shift. (There was no way she was going to get back into that dress.) Hauling back a mound of quilts, Elissa uncovered a riding outfit that she had never worn. Apparently it was not fancy enough to be kept in the storage room with the other garments.

Much to Elissa's relief, the riding costume was not complicated, though she thought it much too elaborate for sitting on a horse. She investigated the skirts and undergarments for hidden traps—hooks, ties, buttons—wondering why anybody would want to dress up to such a ridiculous extent for a horse. The only thing horses really cared about was other horses—who did not need to wear outlandish outfits to make an impression on one another. She wriggled into the pleated skirts, vest, and padded jacket, twisting herself around to adjust the various fasteners. Then she donned a pair of boots and poked her head out the door. The coast was clear. Elissa walked down the hallway trying to look confident. If anyone saw her, she would simply tell them she was going to the stables. They would assume she was going riding, a common morning activity among nobles.

The stables were located near the northern end of the castle grounds, next to the barracks.

Elissa was familiar with the route, as she had taken it often. The frequency with which she visited the stables had led some members of the court to believe her an enthusiast of the hunt, which she definitely was not. Elissa's purpose in visiting the stables was not to select a riding steed, but to visit her donkey and oldest friend, Gertrude.

Unfortunately, Gertrude was not to be found in the stables. Elissa paced the aisle next to her stall, wondering where she might be. It was still early in the day, so perhaps she had been led out to pasture. Elissa left the stables and proceeded to walk alongside the castle walls until she found the gate that led to the pastures. It was guarded by a gentle young man who reminded Elissa somewhat of Han, Bruno's stableboy.

"Planning to take a ride, Your Highness?" asked the guard. "The horses and pack animals are out to pasture this morning, but I'll get a stablehand to bring a horse in for you if you'd like."

"No, thank you," she replied. "I'll find one myself."

The young man opened the gate and smiled

warmly, as all the servants did when they saw Elissa. For unlike the rest of the court, Elissa was always courteous. But more important, she was a completely accessible person. "She's comfortable," the servants often commented. "Like one of us."

"Old Oak has been asking after you," the guard said as he closed the gate behind her. "If you don't mind, Highness."

Oak was in charge of the castle gardens. Though he was in his sixties, he was as strong and tall as his namesake. His daughter Fern had been having trouble with her newborn babe, a problem that Elissa had learned of while over-hearing a conversation between the young serving maids. It was strange, but the servants were remarkably free in what they said while they worked, even though the nobles might be standing right in front of them. Elissa's maids gossiped incessantly while dressing her and tending to her hair, for example. The nobles simply remained silent, as though temporarily deaf. For that reason, the dressing maid, Florie, had been completely shocked when Elissa had suggested that Fern take a three-mint tea to help relieve her infant's colic. Nevertheless, it appeared as if that information had been passed along, for now Oak was asking after her.

"I'll stop by to see him on the way back," said Elissa.

The young man nodded. "I'll pass the word along to Oak." Normally, servants were fetched to the castle, not the other way around. But it was not the role of a servant to question the wishes of nobility, only to fulfill them.

Once through the gate, Elissa scanned the pasture, looking for a lumpy brown shape. Gertrude wasn't hard to find. She was standing at the far end of the pasture near a copse of poplar trees, neatly cropping the luxuriant grass that grew there, her two front hooves planted in a proprietary fashion upon the rich green turf. Gertrude had a knack for locating the greenest, thickest patches of grass.

As Elissa crossed the pasture, she was struck by the hopelessness of her situation. She was no match for a king! Falk would get his way, as he always did. He had power, authority, and the full force of tradition on his side. And she was nothing but a dressed up peasant—one who was about to pour her heart out to a donkey. If her father knew she talked to animals, he'd probably think she was crazy. Not that it mattered. It was only too clear that Falk saw her strictly in terms of how she could benefit him. She could be stark raving mad and it wouldn't change his plans a bit.

Elissa's breath suddenly caught in her throat. A surge of anger ran through her, and her hands tightened into fists. If she had her way, she would simply put an end to all of it—the machinations, the manipulation, the twittering behind her back. Something traveled upward along her spine, spreading through her chest, encompassing her, joining her to something *vast*.

The ground trembled beneath her feet.

Elissa looked up. Were the trees at the edge of the pasture leaning toward her? And was the ground beginning to ripple, as if something were writhing beneath it?

*No!* she thought. *Be as you were!* Elissa took a deep breath, forcing herself to relax. She looked up at the clear blue sky. A bird winged past, trilling. She closed her eyes for a moment, collecting herself. Controlling her thoughts was hard enough, but controlling her emotions was proving to be impossible. Unfortunately, the things of the earth—the creatures, the plants, the very stuff of Nature—responded to both. They did her bidding, even when she had no clear idea what her bidding was. She opened her eyes slowly, keeping her mind and heart focused, self-contained. When the surge was completely gone, she knew she had successfully blocked herself off; danger was averted. Elissa held very still for a while, momentarily drained. The effort of repressing her desires, of thwarting the power that coursed through her, left her feeling limp, and somehow weakened. She waited for her energy to return— as it always did—and then, restored, she hurried to Gertrude and, as she had done since she was a little girl, flung both arms around the donkey's neck.

"Ack!" said Gertrude. "Let go!"

Elissa released her grip. "Gertrude," she said softly. She glanced at the trees, checking for movement. Not even a leaf twitched in the mild spring air. "I have to talk to you." The donkey raised her gray muzzle suspiciously, and swished her tail.

"Don't tell me we're going on another trip," said Gertrude. "I'm not getting on any more boats!"

"No," assured Elissa. "No more boats."

"That's good," said Gertrude. "I'm still seasick from that last trip. It took months to get my figure back." The donkey started to amble off.

"Gertrude!" hissed Elissa. "This is serious. My father is going to marry me off to some awful lord!" Elissa breathed deeply, trying to remain calm.

"You mean he wants to breed you? Foaling's not so bad," said Gertrude. She lowered her head to nip at a tuft of grass.

Elissa sighed. She should have known better than to start this kind of conversation with Gertrude. Donkeys simply did not understand romance. For that matter, neither did Elissa, but she felt that romance was an important consideration when choosing a mate, even if she did not really comprehend how it worked on a practical level. Obligations and duties seemed so often to conflict with love; how did a person manage to keep things straight?

"I have to *care* about the person I'm getting married to," explained Elissa.

Gertrude thought for a moment. "Sort of like me and Ralph," she said.

"Precisely," rumbled a voice.

Elissa felt a warm, moist breath against her neck. "Oh, Ralph!" She looked up into the camel's gorgeous eyes. "I didn't hear you."

"My apologies if I startled you, but I could not help but overhear the topic of your conversation. Did someone mention breeding? Good breeding is *so* important."

"No, Ralph," said Elissa, with a patience she did not feel. "We were talking about the fact that my father wants to marry me off to one of his dreadful cousins."

"Ah," said Ralph. "The blissful state of matrimony!" He winked broadly at Gertrude.

If Elissa wasn't absolutely positive that a donkey was incapable of blushing, she could have sworn . . .

"Back off!" Gertrude exclaimed. "When I'm ready, I'll let you know."

"Of course, Gertie," murmured Ralph. "I wouldn't think of rushing you. And now I will allow you two ladies your tête-à-tête."

Gertrude snorted in derision, but Elissa noticed that she kept her eyes fixed on Ralph as he ambled off. "So," said Gertrude at last. "Who do you want to breed with? Just tell your father who you'd prefer and that will be that."

Elissa chewed on a piece of grass. "It's not quite that simple," she said. "He wants me to marry someone who will make life better for *him*, not somebody who will make life better for *me*." Gertrude could always be counted on for a sympathetic ear, but sometimes it was hard to explain human things to her. People didn't seem to make a lot of sense to Gertrude. Come to think of it, people didn't make a lot of sense to Elissa, either. They killed one another over trifles, pawned their children to gain political power, and mortgaged the future of their grandchildren, all for the sake of controlling a little bit of land. And they wore *really* uncomfortable shoes.

"Hey, at least nobody nails them to your feet," said Gertrude. Elissa didn't realize she had been mumbling out loud.

"Sorry," said Elissa. "I'm just upset."

Gertrude nuzzled her neck. "Don't worry," she said. "You'll figure something out. You always do."

"Thanks, Gertrude," said Elissa without much enthusiasm.

"Maybe you should talk to Maya about this," suggested Gertrude. "At least she's one of your species . . . more or less."

"Maya's just a child," said Elissa. "She wouldn't understand."

"And you think *I* do?" asked Gertrude incredulously.

"You've got a point," said Elissa without rancor. Donkeys were . . . well, donkeys.

"I'll take you down to the shore if you don't want to walk," offered Gertrude.

Elissa realized Gertrude was being unusually generous, for she rarely offered anybody a ride. "No, I'll walk," she replied. The path that led to the shore was not difficult, or long. "I need to think."

As Elissa walked down to the sea, she thought about what Gertrude had said. Choosing a suitor herself would certainly solve the problem. She would be wed and her father would be happy. The only drawback to that particular solution was that she didn't want to marry anybody at all. She wondered if that were possible—*not* to marry.

Maya was not on the shore, where she usually

could be found sunning herself on a smooth rock. Ever since they had arrived at Castlemar, Maya could hardly be dragged from the shore. Nearly every morning, while Elissa was being painstakingly dressed, Maya dashed down to the sea— even in the most inclement weather—and stayed there until close to lunchtime. Elissa counted the little girl as fortunate. For one thing, they let Maya wear her comfortable, free-flowing desert robes. And for another, nobody paid any attention to a child. Maya could go where she liked and do as she pleased. Elissa, in marked contrast, always had the nagging feeling that wherever she went, she was being watched.

Elissa lifted her hand to shade her eyes as she gazed out to sea. Far, far out, among the waves, she spotted a small brown head. She waved both arms and called, even though she knew the wind would snatch her voice away long before it reached Maya's ears. Nonetheless, the head turned and Maya waved back.

Then she disappeared.

Elissa counted the seconds. When she reached sixty, she picked up a pebble. By the time she spotted Maya's head bobbing back up among the breakers, she held seven pebbles in her hand.

Within moments Maya came careening out of the sea, shouting with laughter. Elissa regarded her joyous face and was suddenly reminded of the first time she had met Maya. She'd shoved the little girl into the bathing pool at the Citadel as a prank, and Maya, completely unfazed, had bobbed right back up with her happy, shining eyes, those plump cheeks, that sleek brown body. *She hasn't changed a bit*, marveled Elissa.

"Good morning!" called Maya.

"How can you swim in that surf?" asked Elissa. That morning, the tide was high and the waves pounded like thunder. "It's freezing!"

"It's fun!" said Maya.

Elissa couldn't reply to that. Her idea of fun didn't include drowning—not that Maya ever could.

"Is it time for lunch?"

"Just about," said Elissa, smiling to herself. Like Gertrude, Maya was always willing and able to eat. "Walk me up?"

The little girl threw on her robe and followed

Elissa to the path. Normally, Elissa would spend a relaxing hour with her, gathering shells and sea stones or investigating tide pools.

"What's wrong?" Maya asked as they reached the top of the bluff. "You look sad."

Elissa stood looking out at the blue sea, escaped strands of hair blowing softly around her face. She had not wanted to burden little Maya with her problems, but Maya's sweet smile and kind brown eyes broke Elissa's resolve.

Elissa told her everything. "Men of power are all alike," she concluded, her voice harsh. "My father is no better than the Khan."

Maya rolled her eyes. "You *can't* mean that," she said.

Elissa quieted her bitter thoughts for a moment and pictured the grotesque Khan. "Perhaps I am overstating things a bit."

Maya shivered. "*Nobody* is as bad as the Khan."

"Not even my opportunistic, uncaring, unfeeling father?"

Maya shook her head emphatically. "Not even him."

They were silent for a moment, watching the

thrust and pull of the waves. Maya gazed out to sea with a faraway expression. "It sounds like he doesn't know what he wants," she said.

"What do you mean?" asked Elissa. "He sounded pretty sure of himself to me—'Marry my cousin and secure my southern border.' That's clear enough."

"No, I mean, he doesn't really know what he wants from you," Maya continued. "He wants you to be a princess and do your duty, and he wants you to be his daughter and feel happy. He probably thinks he's doing the right thing."

"Well, he isn't," said Elissa, with a definitive toss of her head.

"I suppose you've already told him that." Maya cocked an eye at Elissa.

"I'm afraid so—though not in so many words."

"What did you do?" asked Maya suspiciously.

Elissa looked away. Now that the moment had passed, she felt a little embarrassed. "I threw my shoes at him. Sort of."

Maya giggled. "Bad mistake," she said. "Now he'll accuse you of having *cold feet*."

Elissa grimaced. "You're as bad as Ralph," she

said. Although she had to admit that kicking her shoes at the King had probably not been the best way to make a point.

"Maybe you should try talking to him again later, when he has settled down," Maya suggested.

Maya was right, of course. Elissa always marveled at how such a young child could be so wise, for Maya was always right. She would wait until her father had cooled off; then she would speak to him again. Perhaps he would be more reasonable later, or at least consider her perspective. After all, he had loved her mother. He, of all people, should understand that marriages must not be forced.

"Let's stop at Oak's cottage on the way back," said Elissa. "He wants to see me."

Maya was more than happy to stop at the gardener's cottage. It was a cheerful place, filled with riotous children and clucking chickens, and presided over by Oak's luminous daughter Fern. Oak had many children, but Fern, with her rosy cheeks and bright smile, was the apple of his eye. Fern had a house of her own, but when her sailor husband was away on extended voyages she moved in with her father, both to keep him company and to take the sting out of her own loneliness.

Elissa approached Oak's cottage in a state of happy anticipation. With its drooping thatched roof and climbing roses, it reminded her of home. She clapped her hands at the outside gate to let Oak know that she had arrived. Within a few moments he appeared, beaming.

"Your Highness!" he cried. "Such a pleasure!"

Elissa would never in her entire life get used to being called "Your Highness," but she accepted Oak's greeting graciously, offering him her hands. "Maya came, too. Is that all right?" she asked. She knew that as Princess, she didn't really need to ask permission for anything, but she wanted to be polite.

"Of course, of course." The old man chucked Maya under the chin, which made her giggle. "Fern will have a treat for ye. Now, Blossom, Pansy, Birch—make way for the Princess!" Oak gently pushed three towheaded children out of the path, where they had been wrestling with a puppy. The children laughed and scampered off, not in the slightest bit impressed by Elissa's title.

*Nor should they be,* Elissa thought.

They entered the cottage, where a soup pot was bubbling merrily on the fire. Elissa breathed in the homey odors: woodsmoke, baking bread, and sweet straw. Fern entered the room. She was a tall, statuesque woman, with golden hair and eyes the color of the sea.

"Princess," she said, making a deep curtsy. Elissa took Fern by the hand and drew her up.

"That's not necessary," she said, even though she knew it was. No commoner would ever fail to bow or curtsy before her. Nor would any call her by her name.

"I wanted to thank ye myself, Your Highness," she said. "I would never have thought of mixing those herbs, but it has worked like magic. The baby's sleeping soundly, and she hardly cries at all."

"I am happy to hear that," replied Elissa, genuinely pleased.

"Will ye take some refreshment with us?" Even though Oak's larder must be spare, it would be rude to refuse Fern's hospitality.

So they sat at the hearth, and ate some of Fern's apple pastries and sipped at Oak's cider, chatting amiably about the weather and the crops, as country people will, until Elissa rose, saying it was time to go.

"Princess," said Oak. "Would ye like to take a look at my wee saplings before ye go?" Oak held his hand out but did not look at her, as if he were afraid she would refuse.

The last time Elissa had visited Oak, he had shown her his apple trees. She had touched each trunk in appreciation as he named the species and described the type of apple each tree produced.

"Of course, Oak," replied Elissa. "I'd love to." It seemed Old Oak enjoyed showing her his plantings. The feeling was mutual, as she enjoyed walking through his orchard as well. It reminded her so much of High Crossing in the spring, when the valley floor was a tapestry of color.

Oak and Elissa walked through the rows of plum, peach, and cherry saplings, Elissa admiring and touching the slender trunks while Oak smiled and smiled. Then they returned to the cottage, where Elissa had left Maya playing with Fern's children. She found her in a tangle of children and puppies, giggling hysterically, while Fern sat under the eaves, laughing. Fern was holding the baby in her lap.

"She's woken up," said Fern. "See how quiet she is?"

"Yes. She seems quite calm," agreed Elissa. Nana's three-mint tea always worked like a charm. "What will you name her?"

Fern cast her eyes down while Oak shifted from one foot to the other. It was bad luck to speak of names before the baby's first two years had passed. Among his people, these were known as "the twain," the two most dangerous years in a child's life, during which any cough, chill, or fever might carry it off to the Underworld. If an infant were to die before the twain was over, a single mention of its name would prevent it from passing into heaven. It would wander the earth forever, a pitiful little spirit looking for its mother. But the Princess had asked, and so Oak must answer.

"We're thinking of naming her Iris, after her grandmother." Oak's eyes grew sad. He missed his wife, as well as the poor wee babe who had died soon after her. His last-born daughter would have been a comfort to him in his old age. All at once, he took the baby from Fern's arms.

"Hold her, Princess!" he said. There was a

note of urgency in his voice that Elissa did not understand, but she took the baby in her arms without protest. The infant's delicate face peeked out from her swaddling cloths, curious to see who now held her. Elissa sighed and gazed at the tiny mouth, the clear blue eyes. When she was Nana's apprentice, she had attended many births and held many a newborn, but never had she seen one so beautiful.

"She's going to look just like her mother," said Elissa, smiling.

Oak looked like he was going to weep with joy. He nodded at his daughter. "All will be well," he exclaimed happily. "All will be well!"

It was this peaceful scene that Favian witnessed as he approached the gate—Old Oak, his face suffused with joy, Fern smiling contentedly, and Elissa tenderly holding a newborn in her arms. He had meant to announce his presence immediately, but hesitated before clapping. Something in Elissa's expression—her sweet tranquility, her ease—made him pause. He took in the humble thatch-roofed cottage, the smell of the woodfire, the tumbling children, and Elissa, bathed in golden sunlight and framed by red and white roses.

Impulsively, and against all protocol, he addressed her by name.

"Elissa!" he called. She turned and smiled at him, an open, welcoming smile that came straight from her heart.

"Come in, come in," cried Oak. His pleasure at receiving friends of the Princess was genuine.

"How did you find me?" asked Elissa, carefully handing the baby back to Fern.

"Aldric told me you were here," explained Favian.

"How did he know where I was?" inquired Elissa.

"Aldric always knows where you are," said Favian. "It's his job." Favian was beginning to look impatient, so Elissa took her leave of Oak's family, thanking them warmly for their hospitality. The fact was, she hated to go.

As Elissa and Favian walked along the high pasture leading back to the castle, Maya scampered on ahead. "See you later!" she cried. Maya did not express any dislike toward Favian, but whenever he was present she managed to disappear. In any event, it was clear that Favian was eager to tell Elissa something in private, so it was just as well that Maya not stay with them.

"I have news!" announced Favian.

"So do I," said Elissa. All at once, she had the urge to confide in Favian. It was an urge she hadn't felt since they had been stuck in Gravesport together. Perhaps it was hearing her name come from his lips. Very few people still addressed her simply as "Elissa," and each one of them held a special place in her heart. "But you tell yours first."

Favian pulled a letter from the inside of his jacket and waved it jubilantly at Elissa.

"My half brothers have finally done it! They have finally managed to get themselves killed! Leonne is mine again. I'm to return immediately."

# ❧ 3 ❧

# The Forbidden Room

On the morning Favian set forth for Leonne, the entire court turned out to see the young count on his way. Favian looked quite dashing in his burgundy velvet cape and jeweled sword. He had refused Falk's generous offer of a contingent of soldiers, claiming that he would travel faster alone. King Falk marked the occasion by wearing his formal robes of state and golden crown. He was accompanied by Aldric, his former Captain of the Guard and current Chief Advisor. Elissa stood apart from them, between her two companions, Maya and Aesha. As they took their places, Aldric greeted Elissa formally, inclining his head gravely. Elissa nodded in return, which was more of an acknowledgment than she had given anyone else that morning. Maya kept very close to Elissa's side. Although Elissa had said nothing to her, Maya knew she was deeply distressed. Aesha, having descended from her quarters to see Favian off, also stood close to Elissa, the Windsinger's little gray bird, Sweetheart, resting on her shoulder. She had a vague awareness that Favian's departure was a significant event, though she did not understand why he was leaving. Aesha was too far removed from the rest of the world to place any importance on the departures of others. However, she realized that a bond was being broken, and that she should bear witness.

Naturally, the Cousins were in attendance as well, fully decked out for the occasion in ribbons and veils, high-backed combs, and stilt-like shoes. They sighed in unison as the gallant young count mounted his horse to the accompaniment of cheers from the Royal Guard. Favian was a popular man.

As Favian called his farewells to the crowd, Rayna drew near and pressed a lock of dark hair into his hand. "To remember me by!" she cried, dabbing at her eyes with a delicate lace handkerchief. Lavinia and Vanna, however, stole some of her thunder by repeating the romantic gesture in rapid succession. "Remember us!" they called.

Graciously, Favian twined all three locks into his belt, causing the Cousins to twitter and swoon.

"He'll never be able to tell them apart," muttered Elissa. Her cousins annoyed her, but at some level she was sorry she had not done the same. More than anyone else, Elissa wanted to be remembered by the young man with the flashing eyes and hands that never grew cold.

King Falk lifted his hand in farewell, along with the rest of his court. "Good luck!" he called. *Good luck and goodbye.* Falk glanced out of the corner of his eye, trying to locate Elissa. But she had disappeared.

During all the shouting and hubbub, Elissa had quietly retreated. The frenetic banner-waving and exuberant cheers had provided sufficient distraction to allow her to escape. Unnoticed by the guards, she made her way up to the battlements atop the western wall. There she stood, watching Favian until he and his horse had long since vanished over the thin blue line of the distant horizon.

In the days that followed Favian's departure, Elissa was constantly nagged by a feeling that something was amiss. It was somewhat like having one's hair combed in the wrong direction, or losing a tooth—as if something that she had formerly taken for granted was now uncomfortably altered. The undercurrent of discomfort that permeated Elissa's mood caused her to be unusually pensive, to the point where Maya was becoming concerned about her.

"What is bothering you?" Maya asked one day as they sat quietly contemplating the sea from Maya's favorite rock.

"I don't know," Elissa confessed. "I just feel that something is wrong. I wake up every morning thinking that I have to do something important, but I can't think of what it might be." What she didn't convey to Maya was that her dreams echoed her feelings. Every night it seemed she dreamt that she had misplaced her little pouch that contained the shard she'd found on the shores of the Sacred Lake, or lost Gertrude or Maya somewhere in the desert. Sometimes she had horrible nightmares that she had been captured by the one-eyed man and locked in a cage, or that Nana was dead. Ironically, the one person who never made an appearance in her dreams was Favian, the only one who was actually gone.

"Let's go do something," suggested Maya, thinking that perhaps Elissa was bored. "Something different."

"Like what?" By now Elissa had done nearly everything Castlemar had to offer a fledgling princess—except marry.

"I don't know," said Maya, shrugging her shoulders. "There must be something."

Elissa thought for a moment or two; then she smiled as an idea struck her. "Let's go to the library," she said. Elissa was proud of the fact that she could now read, a skill she had mastered in record speed, and which she liked to show off.

"Books," said Maya unenthusiastically. The little girl could speak a dozen languages, but all of Elissa's attempts to teach her how to decipher script had failed. A trip to the library was not precisely Maya's idea of a good time.

"Don't look so glum," said Elissa. "We're going to look at some pictures."

Maya immediately brightened. "With colors?" Maya loved anything bright.

The two girls made their way easily to the top of the bluff overlooking the beach, and turned briefly to enjoy the view. The ocean was unusually tranquil that day, and except for a lone ship making its way to the harbor, there was no sign of human activity. Now that Elissa had become accustomed to the sea, with its tumultuous shoreline and vastness of the soundless depths, it no longer frightened her. Perhaps that was because Maya felt so at home there.

The girls entered the castle gate nearest the stables, which Elissa preferred over the other entrances, largely because the young guard never said a word to them. As always, he let the girls pass through the gate quickly and quietly, tacitly offering his cooperation in their morning routine. They climbed the steep, winding stairs of the northeastern tower and reached the library without encountering a soul. There they opened the door cautiously, for if the Librarian was on duty, and awake, he would not let Maya enter. "No children allowed!" he would certainly cry, banging his staff hollowly on the wooden floor. "Sticky hands!"

Elissa, however, had timed their visit well, for it was the Librarian's naptime. The high-backed velvet chair in which he usually sat was empty. The girls tiptoed into the room.

The library consisted of a large vaulted chamber entirely lined with shelves, upon which countless leather-bound books were neatly stacked. The chamber was illuminated by three large leaded windows, under which were placed several small tables. The illuminators and scribes—sharp-eyed young monks, for the most part—preferred to work in the morning, when the light was diffuse and clear and did not distort the colors. Elissa had often seen them there, surrounded by their pens and brushes and pots of ink, working with the full devotion of their calling. Laboriously they copied each word, often enhancing the originals by providing wonderfully elaborated drawings. Elissa delighted in the golden curlicues tipped with animal heads; the tiny people climbing up and down the letters; the magical beings, flowers, vines, fruits. As it was already noon, the tables were empty. Maya and Elissa were completely alone.

Elissa closed the door behind them and hurried Maya through the central chamber—past the tables and chairs, over which some of the monks had draped their coarse outer robes and hoods, and beyond the shelves of musty tomes and ancient leather-bound texts—to a door that had been closed, and padlocked, every time Elissa had visited the library.

"What's in there?" asked Maya, curious.

"It's the map room," said Elissa. The idea of exploring the castle's map room hadn't really occurred to Elissa until today. Her father had told her quite plainly on her first trip to the library that the map room was "not suitable for young girls," and therefore would have to remain locked. Not that she had been interested at the time. However, now that Favian had left Castlemar—had left *her*—she had the sudden desire to see where he had gone; to locate Leonne, at least in her mind's eye. She knew it was the right thing to do, because as soon as she thought of it, her malaise lifted. Elissa removed her hairpin, preparing to pick the lock. To her surprise, it was already sprung. "That's odd," she said in a hushed voice. Elissa held the hairpin in her hand, as if she might need it for something else. Peering into the empty room, she was reluctant to enter. Somehow, finding the door unlocked made her more cautious than if it had been securely bolted.

"Why do they lock it?" asked Maya. She could not understand the relevance, much less the importance, of anything on paper.

Elissa hushed Maya and gently pushed her inside the forbidden room, closing the narrow door carefully after them.

"Maps are for waging wars," she explained, pushing the pin back into her hairnet. "The more accurate they are, the easier it is to plan battle strategy. So they are kept locked up."

Elissa surveyed the map room. It was a fairly small chamber, lined with dark wooden cabinets and dominated by a large square table set under tall windows. There were no shelves at all. Elissa wondered where the maps were kept, until she noticed that the cabinet fronts were studded with tiny knobs. On closer examination, each set of knobs corresponded to a narrow drawer.

"They must be stored in here," she said, approaching the first cabinet. She pulled the top set of knobs and the drawer slid open. Inside it were perhaps half a dozen tight scrolls laid side by side, each one bound with a black satin ribbon. She undid one of the ribbons and looked at the map briefly. "Eastern Holdings," she read.

East was not what she wanted. Leonne lay to the west.

"Look!" cried Maya. "I found the pictures." The little girl was delightedly waving a yellowed scroll at Elissa. She held a faded brown ribbon in her other hand.

"Let's see what you've got," said Elissa, rescuing the scroll from Maya's enthusiastic fist and spreading it out. She held the curling sides of the parchment down with some of the smooth glass weights that were scattered over the surface of the table.

The map was ancient and cracked in places, but it was beautifully drawn. At the top, two words had been inscribed in flowing old-fashioned letters: *The World.* The margins had been filled with fanciful drawings of animals and people in ancient garb, which must have been meant to portray the beings inhabiting all the parts of the earth. In each corner, a seraph puffed out its angelic cheeks to represent one of the four winds.

"What is it saying?" asked Maya, bending her ear down to the paper. Elissa smiled. When she had made her initial attempt to teach Maya to read, Elissa had told her that writing was like speaking, believing that because Maya was so adept at languages, she should be able to transfer her skill. Ever since then, Maya had been convinced that script talked in a language that only Elissa could understand, much as only Elissa understood Gertrude and all the other animals.

"It says that this is the world," explained Elissa, pointing to the principal recognizable features of the map. She placed her finger at the top of the scroll, where the Great Circle was depicted by a crown of snowcapped peaks. "Look here. This is the top of the world." Beneath the Circle stretched a wide blue area bounded by uneven black lines. Elissa traced the edge of the sea with the tip of her finger.

"Is it saying anything about us?" asked Maya, gazing intently at Elissa's finger.

"No, we are too small," said Elissa quietly. "This is the whole world."

Indeed it was. All the holdings, the eastern kingdoms, the southern desert lands, the northern valleys and mountains, and the rugged lands of the Western Reach were neatly drawn and labeled, each with its most prominent geographical features—mountains, rivers, plains, and forests.

"Do you want to see where we have been?" asked Elissa. She pointed to a spot in the southwest, where there was a drawing of a fortress set in a flat expanse of dull brown. "That is the Citadel of the Khan."

"It looks just like it!" exclaimed Maya. Indeed, the drawing quite accurately represented the blunt, red-hued walls of the Citadel.

"We traveled south and east," said Elissa, drawing her finger to where the desert ended and a blue thread wound its way down from the mountains. "Here is the Serena River, and here are the swamps." On the map, the lowlands, richly colored in deep green, were quite extensive. Elissa hadn't realized they made up most of the southern territories. The desert also looked considerably smaller than it had felt when they had crossed it. She peered at the map. The green area extended some distance from Alhamazar, much farther than it should. Ralph had been right. The desert had indeed grown. If this map were to be drawn again today, there would hardly be any green at all above the great city. She moved her finger along the blue line of the Serena, to a dark splotch on the coastline.

"This is Gravesport," she said. Then she followed the line up the coast, north and east. "And here is Castlemar." She pointed to a drawing of a many-turreted castle on the shore. "Home."

"Show me your real home," said Maya.

As always, Maya managed to cut straight to the truth.

In spite of all Elissa's wishful thinking, Castlemar would probably never be her "home," not in the way High Crossing had been. Soberly, Elissa examined the area to the north and west of Castlemar until she found a valley between two mountain ranges, bisected by a thin blue line.

"This must be High Crossing," she murmured. The shape of the terrain was familiar to her, as were the wavy lines, though she had never seen a map of High Crossing before. Looking at the brown lines of the mountains and the broad green bowl of the valley, Elissa briefly wondered why she had ever wanted to leave Bruno's tranquil holding. Had she simply been bored? Had she grown tired of the winding river, the lush pastures, the high mountain meadows and plummeting falls? The valley had seemed so limited.

Now, with the world spread beneath her hand, her finger tracing her journeys over the desert and through the lowlands, down the Serena and up the shore of the Great Sea, the world seemed so much smaller than it had been. Less filled with possibilities.

Elissa sighed, unable, for the moment, to articulate her sense of loss—of her homeland and . . . What? She didn't really know. Elissa continued her search to the west—mountains and more mountains. Where was Leonne? She moved her finger south until she came to what looked like a patch of brown bumps. The words "Western Provinces" were inscribed in a long, straggling line beneath the whole bumpy area. "This could be Leonne," she said doubtfully.

Maya wasn't paying attention. She was examining another part of the map. "I found *my* home," she announced abruptly.

Maya was waving the tip of her braid over an oddly shaped island drawn in the midst of the great blue area. Elissa peered at it closely, for the lines were very faint. In the center of the island was a forbidding gray fortress, over which hovered an ominous winged creature. *That is the island in the middle of the Great Sea,* Elissa suddenly realized. *The one no traveler can approach . . . without getting eaten.* Elissa shook her head ruefully. She'd always thought the island was one of Nana's myths.

"Is *this* your home?" asked Elissa incredulously, pointing at the island. "Where the monster lives?"

Maya laughed. "No," she said, giggling, "not *there.*" Apparently she hadn't been pointing to the island after all, but somewhere else.

Elissa was about to ask Maya exactly where she meant when she heard a noise.

"Shh." Elissa held her finger to her lips and quickly rolled up the scroll. Silently, she tiptoed to the door and stood close to it, holding her breath. If the Librarian had returned, they might have to wait until he wandered off on some bookish errand in order to sneak out of the room. Sometimes he fell asleep in his chair, however, in which case they would probably be able to slink past him once he dozed off.

"My lord," said a muffled voice.

It was Aldric. Only she and Aldric still called Falk by his old title. Elissa heard an answering voice: her father's. The voices were indistinct, but as she listened, they came closer. She pressed her ear to the door to hear them better.

"I think you are making a mistake," said Aldric.

"How so?"

"She seemed rather fond of the boy."

There was a scraping noise, as if a chair was being moved. "Yes, I admit I was rather fond of him myself, but he had no prospects. Even if he regains his lands, they're worthless."

"He might get killed en route," said Aldric casually.

Elissa's breath caught in her throat.

"Or after reaching Leonne," said Falk, with equal ease. "I wouldn't put it past that viper of a woman to attempt something of the sort. She's certainly caused enough mayhem already in Leonne. But Favian is a survivor."

Aldric grunted an assent. "His skill with the sword will certainly stand him in good stead— that is, if he doesn't run into any of those mystery weapons you told me about. Have you been able to discover any information about the maker?"

"No," said Falk. "My spies have discovered nothing. Either he is very good at hiding or he is dead. In any case, it is to my gain. I may be able to make some of my own, now that I have the model."

There was a pause. "Do you think that is wise, my lord? A weapon that can be easily hidden, requires little skill to operate, and can kill at a safe distance could easily be turned against you. Best to destroy it."

Falk grunted softly, noncommittal.

"War must remain in the hands of competent professionals"—Aldric's voice was solemn—"men who look their enemies in the eye and feel their blood on their hands, or all will be reduced to ashes by headstrong amateurs. Taking lives is serious business, a responsibility not to be taken lightly, or made too easy."

A long silence followed.

"You are right, Aldric," replied Falk at last. "I will leave the matter in your hands."

"Very wise," said Aldric. Then he added in a low voice, "If only you were as wise in family matters."

"What do you mean?" Falk's voice was sharp.

"For one thing, she might not even like Lord Gavin," said Aldric.

"What has that got to do with anything?" retorted Falk. "Once she gets used to him, she will come to care for him. That's why I invited him to spend some time with us before the ball."

"And for another thing," continued Aldric, pursuing his point, "she probably won't react well if you announce her betrothal at the ball. She has not had enough time to weigh the matter. I am almost sure she will balk."

"She is obstinate," replied Falk, "and willful."

"As are you," said Aldric. "Have you considered that by presenting her with no other option, you might be forcing her into acting rashly? After all, she was not raised as you were. It will take her some time to become accustomed to her royal duties and responsibilities."

"That is precisely why I have arranged for her other friends to leave before the ball. As long as they remain here, she will not adjust to her new life. Once they are out of the way, she will come to her senses and finally accept her duties.

Elissa clutched Maya's hand. *Out of the way?*

"Have you forgotten your own history?" Aldric spoke carefully.

"That was different," said Falk curtly. "My

father had absolutely no regard for me. *I* want what is best for Elissa."

There was the sound of footsteps, and Elissa knew Falk was pacing while Aldric, with his long, immobile face, was weighing his next words.

"You need to release your grip on her," said Aldric simply. "While you still can."

"And you need to mind your own affairs!" Falk snapped.

Aldric's reply came after a brief, tense silence. "But you employ me to mind *yours* . . . sire," he said in measured tones.

There was another silence, followed by the sound of a hand slapping a sturdy back, and then Falk's hearty laughter. "And you never let me forget it," he said.

"Do you still want that map?" Aldric asked.

Elissa heard the sound of footsteps approaching the door. She let go of Maya and drew back a few steps. Maya pulled at Elissa's skirt and pointed frantically to the heavy drapes that hung on either side of the window. Elissa shook her head sharply, just once. She was not going to hide from her father this time. When he came through that door, she would be ready for him. Firmly, with her gaze leveled directly in front of her, Elissa stood her ground. Maya backed away from her. She had never seen such a look in Elissa's eyes before. It was fierce, wild.

The door creaked softly as Aldric began to push it open. Elissa tensed.

"No," said Falk. "Let's come back some other time. I am not in the mood to plan strategy right now. Just remember to tell the Librarian to lock up."

"I will," said Aldric.

Elissa could see part of Aldric's shoulder and the edge of his arm through the doorway. If she had wanted to, she could have reached out and touched him.

The door clicked shut. Soon two sets of footsteps could be heard retreating. Then the echoing slam of the heavy library door filled the room.

After they had gone, Elissa remained motionless, facing the door of the map room, the scroll of The World clutched in her right fist—like a weapon.

# ≈ 4 ≈

# A Tranquil Place

Favian kept a steady course westward, the sun warming his back and the foothills of Castlemar's northern range guarding his right flank. Soon the undulating hills that stretched before him would rise into lofty mountains and his straight western course would be deflected. There was no pass that led directly through the mountains at Castlemar's far western boundary, which meant he would have to choose an indirect route to Leonne, and there were only two: the first crossed over the northern pass, and the second led through the Southern Wilderness. The southern route was a little shorter; however, the Wilderness was infested with outlaws, cutthroats, and thieves. For that reason, many travelers who chose the forest route did not arrive at their destination. The northern pass was more circuitous, but safe—and there were settlements along the way to provide Favian and his horse with food and shelter. Favian was eager to arrive home as soon as humanly possible, but he also wished to arrive in one piece. He decided upon the northern pass, gradually turning his mount northward as he made his way across the gently rolling hills of the Eastern Reach.

Curiously, for he had left the castle with a smile on his lips and a song in his heart, he felt increasingly troubled as he distanced himself from Castlemar. The farther he rode, the more tense he became. It was as though he were an arrow straining against the ever-tightening string of an enormous bow, which, when it reached its maximum extension, would fling him, not ahead to his destination, but back to Castlemar. In spite of his joy at being able to return home to claim his birthright, he had to admit that his uncle's summons had produced mixed feelings in him. For one thing, the deaths of his half brothers led him to worry about his reception at Leonne. It was bound to be chilly . . . at best.

Curses have power, and surely his had come to fruition. Would Sonia blame him for her sons' deaths? Even if she didn't hold him directly responsible, he knew that in some way she would make him accountable. This was Sonia's greatest talent in life—the ability to shift responsibility onto someone else's shoulders. Favian supposed it was his stepmother's way of covering her own sin-littered trail. Not that her sly manipulations, false accusations, and feigned ignorance had ever fooled Favian. As a tracker, Favian was without equal. She could not hide her trail of misdeeds from him—that is, if he cared to seek them out. As it happened, he did not. Favian's major grievance against Sonia had occurred a long time ago, too long ago for anyone else to care about. And right now, all he really wanted was to get his home back. Or so he thought. The doubt that intruded upon Favian's mind with increasing strength as he neared his destination was whether the present Leonne, after so many years of Sonia's rule, would conform to what he remembered as "home." He rode hard, as if the possibility that Leonne might not be quite as he had imagined was following in hot pursuit.

Eventually Favian reached the mountains and found respite from his uncomfortable thoughts, for once he started the ascent, Favian was forced to slow his furious pace and focus on the rough terrain. His steed, a mighty bay generously given to him by King Falk, was perhaps not the fastest horse in the royal stables, but it possessed great strength and endurance. In spite of the fact that Favian rode all morning and throughout the afternoon on most days, it showed no signs of tiring. However, in consideration of such a fine beast, Favian slowed his pace even further as the trail grew steep, allowing the horse to rest often. No matter how impatient Favian felt, it would be shameful to ride a horse to death.

When he thought he had nearly reached the summit, Favian stopped by a mountain spring to water the animal and stretch his legs. It was the ideal place for a break. The spring, set in a secluded, softly turfed glade, burbled cheerfully through a crack in the rocks and spilled into a tiny, crystal-clear pool. Favian noticed that the water flowed to the west rather than to the east, which meant they had already crossed the divide. Leaving his horse to drink and graze, he followed a footpath that led away from the glade through a copse of stunted pines. Within a few yards, the narrow path gave out onto a high ledge. The lookout offered a broad view of the valley below. The valley was a perfect green bowl, with mountains to either side and a river passing neatly through the middle—a fertile, sheltered spot. He was not surprised to see that it had been thoroughly settled. Small farms and orchards dotted the entire valley floor. At the center of the valley stood a large house, probably a manor. Favian decided to push on and stay there for the night. He had no fear of being turned away. Nobility always takes care of its own.

He mounted his horse, following the bridle path. After a few minutes it twisted back upon itself and started to descend. Favian smiled in anticipation of the comforts of civilization. Rather than leave the path to seek shelter, he had saved time by sleeping in the open the past few nights. A bed and a hot meal would be welcome. He knew he would find both at the manor. It was a pity he had not had the opportunity to notify the lord in advance. He would have liked to have shown him the courtesy.

As Favian descended into the valley, he was

pleased to see that it looked well tended. It seemed that the drought that had so adversely affected Castlemar, and indeed much of the West and South, had not made as great an impact here. He wove his way alongside moist green fields and shady orchards until the pleasant tree-lined lane widened and led onto the manor grounds proper.

The manor was a simple construction of stone and heavy timber, not ostentatious or elaborate in any way, but large and sturdy—a practical building. Remarkably, it possessed no fortifications whatsoever. Perhaps this valley was so lacking in strategic value or riches that the manor needed no defense. Favian made his way to the main gate, wondering how he might announce himself, there being no guard in sight.

He did not have long to wonder, for he was soon greeted by the lord himself—a large, brown-bearded man in his prime. He wore a plain, unadorned cloak and swordless belt, but the confidence of his stance and the broadness of his shoulders left no doubt that he was none other than the lord of this manor. Beside him stood a tall, fair-haired woman of similar age, and several youths and young ladies who looked so much like the woman that Favian assumed she must be their mother, the lady of the manor.

Favian bowed to them, and introduced himself merely as Favian of Leonne. The rest would come later.

"Welcome to the valley!" cried the lord, extending his hand. "I am Bruno, and this is my dear wife, Hilde, and our children." The lady of the manor took his hand in both of hers, as did the children—each of them grasping Favian's hand in turn and greeting him courteously. Though Favian thought it odd that not one of them bowed or curtsied, he appreciated the warm and obviously heartfelt welcome. They ushered him into the house while a tall youth of gentle demeanor attended to his horse.

From the sweet smell of citron boughs in the rafters and from the fresh rushes on the floor, it appeared that the Manor had been prepared for his arrival. *They must have an efficient and entirely hidden signaling system,* thought Favian, *which probably accounts for the lack of fortifications.* If an enemy were to approach, the whole valley would be forewarned, and prepared, hours before the soldiers arrived. Nevertheless, Favian could not see any reason to attack this pleasant little vale.

"Please refresh yourself," said Lady Hilde. "And when you have rested, do join us in our apartments. Gerta will show you the way." A pretty, if somewhat skinny, child dimpled happily at her task and led Favian up a creaking flight of stairs to his rooms, which, he was pleased to note, were clean and comfortable. Delight of delights, a warm bath had been prepared for him.

After bathing, Favian stretched himself out upon the bed. He was almost tempted to stay there. But it would have been rude to ignore his hosts' invitation to dine with them. Travelers, though they were not expected to pay for their lodgings, were expected to provide news of the world. And Favian had much news to tell.

A timid knock roused Favian. When he opened the door, the child, Gerta, asked him if he was ready to be escorted to Bruno's apartments.

"I am ready," he informed her gravely. "Do you think I shall have need of my sword?" The girl dropped her head shyly, clearly not accustomed to being addressed by strangers.

"No," she replied seriously. "Cook chops up

everything very well with her cleaver." Favian laughed, and thought the child clever until he realized she had answered him with utter sincerity.

They made their way to the lord's chambers, which turned out to be no more elaborate than his own. A fire was blazing in the hearth, for the evening air was chilly in this high valley. Lord Bruno invited Favian to sit at a sturdy wooden table next to the fire and then sat down himself, with his lady at his right side. To his surprise, the children remained, arraying themselves about the room on small chairs and upon stools, as though they ate with their parents every night. Perhaps they did. Favian thought this a most unusual custom. In other manors, the children would have been confined to the nursery at mealtime, well out of earshot of their parents. Hilde's offspring, in apparent ignorance of this type of exile, chattered quietly to one another while Bruno inquired after Favian's comfort. Favian found the piping sounds of the children's voices unexpectedly soothing.

Within a few moments a serving girl appeared, bearing bowls of food upon a large copper tray. She served each of them in no special order. And when she came to Lord Bruno, he thanked her jovially.

"Enjoy your meal!" was the girl's cheery reply. Her manner was so matter-of-fact toward Lord Bruno, it was obvious he thanked her as a matter of course. The girl smiled at Favian as she left.

*What a bizarre place,* thought Favian as he began to eat. Servants who spoke directly to their lords while performing their duties—lords who thanked them! How could one maintain discipline in such an atmosphere? Yet it seemed as though Bruno, his family, and even the servants were all quite comfortable with this arrangement. And the food, though served in rustic ceramic bowls, was delicious.

"This is marvelous, my lord," he said with genuine appreciation.

"I'm glad you like it," said Lord Bruno, smiling. "I'll tell Cook myself. It will please her to know our guest liked her special venison stew. Perhaps," he added with a twinkle in his eye, "she'll make it just for me sometime."

This was a strange place indeed! They finished their meal in a silence that was unbroken except for pleasant and general comments on the meal, the beauty of the gardens this year, the mildness of the season. After the table was cleared—amazingly enough, by the children—Bruno drew Favian closer to the fire, where three comfortable padded chairs had been placed. Favian sighed as he and his hosts settled themselves in. Now that dinner was over, he would be expected to tell his news.

"Where are you bound?" asked Bruno. His face glowed in the aftermath of a good dinner and with the promise of the tale to come, for whatever purpose travelers might have in passing through these parts, there was always a story that lay behind their travels, and it was always entertaining.

"I am bound for Leonne," said Favian. "I am going to be reinstated as its Count." The lord and his lady looked startled. It was clear they were not up to date on the latest news. He told them of his half brothers' demise as best he could, since he was lacking all the details of their deaths, and in broad strokes he recounted his personal story and travels. Bruno and his lady nodded and clucked and showed every sign of enjoyment during his tale. Eventually there was a silence.

"Have you come from Castlemar?" asked Hilde. She was stroking the bright head of one of her sleepy children, who, without a trace of self-consciousness, had crept into her lap.

"Why, yes," answered Favian. "I left the castle hardly a week ago."

"Ah," said Bruno, exchanging a glance with his lady. "We have heard that King Falk has returned with his daughter, the Princess Elissa. Is this true?"

The lord and lady, and all the children, grew silent.

Favian thought for a moment of Elissa. What could he say? He knew less than he should about her. "Yes, he has brought the Princess to Castlemar," he said. Judging from the eager looks on their faces, they probably wanted to hear all about the Princess. She was new at Court, and no doubt had been the topic of much speculation and gossip.

"The Princess is very charming," he began somewhat defensively, as if to lay any rumors to rest. "And she is quite beautiful." *Must not disappoint*, thought Favian. Everyone expected a princess to be beautiful. Of course, in this case it also happened to be true.

Bruno smiled at Favian in such an open and

encouraging way that Favian felt compelled to say more.

"She is a fine person," continued Favian. "Very honest, and . . ." Favian hesitated. He couldn't very well tell them she had saved his life in a swamp. That behavior wasn't very princess-like.

". . . courageous," he continued. "She will make an exceptional queen." Favian couldn't think of what else to say.

Bruno and Hilde exchanged a look that Favian could not interpret. They both seemed pleased, though not as much as Favian would have thought. Usually, intimate contacts with royalty impressed minor lords to no end.

"But is she happy?" inquired Bruno. "Does her father treat her well?"

Bruno's questions took Favian by surprise. This type of inquiry was completely out of keeping. What did the lord of this remote manor care about a faraway princess? Or her father? The very oddness of the questions prompted him to answer directly.

"Yes," he replied. "I do believe she is happy. The King is quite fond of her, and she has everything she could want." It seemed the best answer, though perhaps not entirely accurate. For as long as he had known her, Elissa had been troubled by something. But since he did not know the nature or the scope of her preoccupations, he could not, and indeed should not, allude to them.

Favian's answer seemed to satisfy his host, for he leaned back into his chair with a sigh and smiled deeply.

"I am glad to hear that," he said. "Very glad."

The fire was flickering low, and after a few more brief questions about Castlemar, Favian's hosts bade him a pleasant evening. Gerta led him back to his rooms, though that was quite unnecessary. Once Favian had traveled a route, he never forgot it.

"Good night," she said, and scampered off. No "sire," no "my lord"; just "good night." At this point, Favian had no idea if she was a servant or another child of the lord's. In this place, it hardly mattered.

Favian threw off his clothes and gratefully crept into bed.

The next morning, Favian was awakened by the sound of birds singing. He rose and dressed in his traveling clothes, as he did not plan on staying another night. Favian stretched his arms and legs, preparing them for another few days in the saddle. The thought came to him that he would like to take a walk before departing. It was still too early for him to say goodbye to his host, and a brief stroll through the gardens would be a pleasant way to start the day. Favian made his way down to the main entrance quietly, so as not to disturb the slumber of his hosts, or anyone else who might still be abed at this early hour. The door, as he suspected, was not locked.

*This is a place that should not reasonably exist,* thought Favian as he began his walk. *Nobody feels this secure.* He followed the path around to the south of the Manor, where he thought the gardens might lie. But instead of gardens, he found a stand of fruit trees leading to a little knoll. Atop the knoll stood a small stone cottage. As there was no smoke drifting upward from the chimney, Favian decided to make a closer inspection of the building and its yard.

As he came around to the front of the cottage he was at first surprised, and then awed, by the utter familiarity of it. Two rose vines twined around the low door frame, above which, like a single furry eyebrow, drooped a deeply thatched roof. If he closed his eyes, he could almost see Elissa standing among the roses, holding a baby in her arms and smiling at him—a wonderful open smile, full of pleasure at hearing him call her name.

"Hello."

Favian had been so absorbed in re-creating his vision of Elissa that he jumped. A pudgy little boy stood behind him, apparently having followed him from the Manor.

"Hello," replied Favian in turn. The boy regarded him pleasantly, his round face creased in a friendly smile. On a whim, Favian ventured a question.

"Who lives here?" he asked. If the boy had replied, "The gardener, Oak," Favian would not have been at all surprised.

"Nobody," said the boy. Favian felt a twinge of disappointment, though he did not know why. It was pure absurdity to expect that Castlemar's gardener might have lived in this cottage. And what did he care who lived here, anyway?

"But there used to be an old woman—a healer—and her granddaughter," the boy continued. "A dark man came one day and took the granddaughter far away, and then the old woman vanished. Nobody knows where she went."

The story sounded intriguing, but Favian did not have the time to pry out the details. In any event, it was unlikely that the boy even knew them. Judging from the unkempt condition of the grounds and the birds roosting contentedly in the thatch, the cottage had stood empty for quite some time. It probably had been abandoned long before this boy was born, and its inhabitants were most likely dead, reduced to a quaint folktale.

Nevertheless, he thanked the child for telling him the story and went back to the Manor. He realized, walking along the narrow path flanking the river, that he would be sad to leave. Bruno's valley was such a tranquil place, and in a strange way, he enjoyed the lack of formality. It reminded him somewhat of the easy camaraderie he'd experienced aboard the *Swamp Maiden*. In fact, with their forthright manners and comfortable acceptance of one another, the people here reminded him of Elissa. Perhaps, one day, he and Elissa might visit Bruno's peaceful valley together. He was sure she would feel right at home.

## ❧ 5 ❧

# Planning Her Escape

Elissa's coming-out ball was to be held in three days' time, and the castle was turning itself inside out for the occasion. The servants had removed nearly all the heavy rugs and tapestries and had beaten them to within an inch of unraveling, knocking out the dust and debris that had gathered there for months—or years, in the case of the tapestries. Even the walls had been thoroughly scrubbed, so much so that they gleamed. In the evening, they reflected the candlelight like mirrors. The kitchen staff was busy polishing silver, the stablehands buffed leather trappings, and the groundskeeper made sure that all the roads leading to the castle were kept clear of fallen branches and rocks. Guests were arriving daily from all parts. The castle absorbed them effortlessly.

Other than allowing herself to be measured for a gown, Elissa took no part in the preparations. Although she was required to spend an hour every afternoon with the Dance Master, she never asked any questions of him, nor did she express any interest in the music, or in the steps, poses, and gestures that were designed to accompany it. From her perpetually glum expression, Elissa might have been preparing to attend a funeral rather than a party, which was, perhaps, closer to the truth. Aldric had informed her just yesterday that both Aesha and Maya would be leaving on the morning of the ball. Their ships were already in the harbor—Aesha's bound for Northport, Maya's for Southport.

Elissa sat disconsolately by her window, gazing out over the plains. Her window faced west, so the morning sun illuminated her room weakly. There were shadows in the corners where cool pockets of night air still clung. Normally she would have been up and about by now, but this morning she felt a lack of will that sapped her of every drop of energy.

Ever since that awful day in the library when she had overheard her father's plan, she had been preparing to do battle with him. However, being inexperienced in conflict, she did not know how to wage her end of the "war." So she had waited for him to make the first move. Yesterday he had made it, and now she could not make a response. For in spite of her dismay at her friends' imminent departure, and at her father's clandestine arrangements for it, she felt that it was entirely reasonable that Aesha and Maya should go home. So many years had passed since Maya had seen her family, they must have given her up for dead. It would be nothing short of cruel to keep her away from her mother any longer. And Aesha, who had passed the last three months patiently waiting for the sea ice to melt around Northport, had been only too pleased to hear that she would soon be returning home. She had expressed her happiness at the news by coming to Elissa's room to offer her thanks personally.

"I hope I haven't appeared ungrateful," Aesha said in her soft, whispery voice.

"Not at all," said Elissa kindly, though the truth of the matter was that Aesha hadn't *appeared* at all. She had hardly seen the Windsinger since Favian had left. Not only had she kept to herself, but even on those rare occasions when Elissa had spoken with Aesha, she had seemed more like a shadow than a person. The solidity that she had seemed to gain on the sea trip to Castlemar had long since ebbed away, leaving Aesha nearly transparent. If it wasn't for the little gray bird that was nearly always perched on her shoulder, Aesha, with her white hair, white skin, and white dress, could be easily mistaken for a phantom. She had become so insubstantial that, at times, Elissa was surprised that she could be seen at all.

"You will always be welcome here," said Elissa warmly.

"Thank you," murmured Aesha. "But I shall not pass this way again. Once I return home, I do not intend to leave the Great Circle." Aesha's mysterious opaque eyes shifted and changed. It was very hard to read them, which is why most people could not meet Aesha's gaze. Elissa, though, always found herself entranced by Aesha's eyes. They revealed the world, or at least a part of it. Now, as Aesha spoke, Elissa thought she saw ice in her eyes, and a great expanse of emptiness.

Aesha's eyes were not fixed on emptiness,

however. Her changeable eyes worked in ways that were peculiar to Windsingers alone, and even though Aesha's eyes betrayed little, they saw much. Now Aesha was watching the air shift and move around Elissa. It moved in great swirling patterns around her, quite unlike the patterns it formed around Favian. From him, the air rose in upward spirals, as if from a flame. Elissa's patterns were majestic, slow, grand. Aesha always felt comforted by Elissa's air. And so she was sorry to say goodbye, though she was not sad to leave. It was her time to go.

"I shall miss you," Aesha said suddenly. Her admission seemed to come as a surprise to Aesha herself, for she immediately excused herself breathlessly. As she floated down the hall and back to her room, Aesha did not know what had led her to say such a thing. The little bird warbled in her ear, calming her.

Elissa thought about Aesha as she sat by her window. It would have been nice to have gotten to know her better, if it was indeed possible for anyone to know Aesha. Though, on reflection, there could have been one exception.

*Maya might be able to know her,* thought

Elissa. Everyone felt comfortable with little Maya. In fact, Elissa felt more comfortable with Maya than with anyone else in the world—aside from Gertrude. The two of them had been through so much together. Elissa sighed heavily. *Oh dear. How on earth am I going to get along without my Water Girl?*

A knock on the door roused Elissa. "Come in," she called, thinking it must be the tailor, here to take more measurements. Her ball gown was already so unbearably complicated, she couldn't conceive that anything more *could* be done to it. Nevertheless, the tailor had expressed a desire to attach yet more lace, more buttons, more layers. Elissa imagined it was going to take her maids all day to get her into it.

Instead of the tailor, it was Aldric who entered. "Princess," he said, bowing briefly.

Aldric was the only person who could address Elissa as "Princess" without causing her to cringe. He was, in fact, the only person in the castle whose bow was genuine. There was no undercurrent of mockery in either the formality of his speech or the courtliness of his gestures. Elissa very much appreciated that, even if she never showed it. She knew Aldric watched her, and then reported what he observed to the King. Elissa was quickly learning how to hide her true intentions.

"The King wishes to see you," Aldric announced.

Elissa frowned. It was out of keeping for the Chief Advisor to be sent on such a menial errand. Undoubtedly, something of significance had happened—or was about to happen. She had a suspicion that her father was ready to initiate the next phase of his battle plan.

Elissa accompanied Aldric quietly down the hall. Elissa was normally quiet, so her silence was not in any way unusual. But lately, Aldric had noticed that Elissa had been excessively silent, which disturbed him. It wasn't just the lack of speech he found alarming, it was her air of deep contemplation. Aldric had misjudged Elissa once, mistaking her silence for docility. He had vowed he would never do so again, and so now, as they made their way to the King's chambers, Aldric resolved to keep a more watchful eye on her, just in case.

When they arrived at Falk's chambers, Aldric

stepped in front of Elissa in order to knock on the door. A servant opened it immediately. Aldric then excused himself, as this was a private audience, and Elissa was ushered into an inner chamber, where King Falk sat in conversation with a man who, judging from his dark hair and neatly trimmed goatee, was obviously a noble.

"Ah, Elissa," said Falk. "I would like you to meet my cousin, Lord Gavin, Duke of Cardys." Elissa approached the man and extended her hand. The Duke rose and bowed formally over Elissa's hand, kissing it lightly. Elissa found the custom of hand-kissing a bit too intimate for her tastes, but had learned to keep her wrist limp and her face expressionless.

"I am pleased to make your acquaintance, Princess," the Duke said cordially, confirming Elissa's initial impression. He was exactly like her father—refined, elegant, restrained. Were it not for his graying temples and the greater girth of his waist, he might have been Falk's twin. "I have heard so much about you."

Elissa never knew what to say when people made comments of that sort. What had they heard? That she had been raised by an old midwife in a remote Northern holding? Or that she had been used as collateral in securing an army for her father? Against this very man, in fact. She guessed that the Duke was probably aware only of those facts her father had deemed necessary for him to know, so she merely nodded her head graciously in reply. To her relief, Gavin invited her to sit. Although the walk had been short, her feet were already aching in her tight shoes. It took several minutes for her to adjust her gown properly, an interim that allowed her to prepare for some small talk. Perhaps she should say something like *How was your trip?* or *Do you like Castlemar?* Except that she imagined he was already quite familiar with Castlemar. After all, he had made plans to conquer it not too long ago. Banal questions were so tedious. Maybe she should say something more direct—for example, *What makes you think you're going to marry me?* His goatee would probably fall off. Elissa composed her face into a pleasant expression and decided to say nothing.

"Your ball is going to be magnificent," Gavin said with enthusiasm. "I am very much looking forward to it. In fact, I have every intention of monopolizing you all evening, if you will permit me to be your partner."

Was he asking for permission to monopolize her? What was she supposed to say to that? *No, I'd rather distribute myself evenly among all the guests, just in case anybody else wants a bite.* Gods, she was beginning to feel like a main course! Elissa smiled vaguely at the Duke's chin. She noticed that his goatee was waxed.

Falk smiled apologetically. "The Princess has been subjected to daily torture by our Dance Master. I am afraid she is not fond of the dance."

Gavin regarded her steadily, not in the least bit put off. Elissa had the impression that, like her father, he was used to being in control. "Well, in that case, we will just sit and talk." He lifted his eyebrows at Falk, as if to say, *She does talk, doesn't she?*

Elissa steeled herself and replied, "That would be lovely."

Falk nodded smugly at his cousin and quickly engaged Gavin in a discussion of the ball, the musicians, the dinner, and who was expected to come. Elissa sat quietly while they talked, knowing full well that the conversation was for her benefit. Gavin already knew who would be there—and everything else, too. As soon as there was a brief lull in the conversation, she excused herself, saying that she had a fitting for her ball gown.

"Until this evening," said Gavin. Apparently they were going to dine together.

After Elissa had gone, Gavin turned to Falk.

"She will do very well," said the Duke, beaming. "I prefer a quiet wife."

When Elissa returned to her room, she found Maya sitting on a chair by the window.

"What are you doing here?" asked Elissa. "I thought you were taking a swim."

"I decided to wait for you instead," said Maya. They both knew that their days together were numbered. "So? What happened? Florie told me you were talking with your father and some kind of noble." It seemed the maids always knew everything long before anybody else.

"Ugh," said Elissa.

"Is he very hideous?" Maya screwed up her face.

"No," replied Elissa with resignation. "He looks like my father, only a little older."

"Older?" Maya looked incredulous. "You'll have to prop him up with a broom to dance with him."

Elissa sat down in the chair opposite Maya's. "I'm not going to dance with anybody. I'm not going to the ball," she said abruptly. She hadn't really intended to make such a firm pronouncement, but as soon as the words left her mouth, she realized that in some inner recess of her mind, she had been planning her escape for a while. Now that she had actually voiced it, her gloom abruptly lifted. In fact, she felt rather happy at the prospect of not attending her own ritual sacrifice.

Maya inched her chair closer to Elissa's and whispered, "What are you going to do? Are you going to hide somewhere so they can't find you?"

"Actually," said Elissa. "I'm going with you."

Maya clapped her hands together. "Oh!" she cried. "That's wonderful! Is your father letting you come home with me?"

"No," said Elissa carefully. "Not exactly. Listen, I have an idea."

Maya listened attentively while Elissa spoke. Once Elissa had made the decision to leave, the rest seemed simple. She only hoped her escape would be as easy to carry out as it was to plan. It must go without a hitch, for once she had left, she had no intention of returning to Castlemar.

On the morning of the ball, Elissa bade farewell to both Aesha and Maya with every appearance of regret. A carriage was waiting in the courtyard to take them to the harbor, where the *Northern Star* and the *Southern Cross* were moored, ready to carry them in opposite directions. She clasped Aesha gently by the hand and wished her a safe journey. Then she hugged Maya close to her.

"Don't forget to feed Gertrude plenty of fresh grass," said Elissa in a loud whisper. "She doesn't like stale greens." Then she flung her arms around Gertrude and sniffed dramatically.

Gertrude hmphed in disgust and said, "Don't ham it up! You'll wreck everything!" Fortunately, nobody else could understand her . . . except for Ralph, who was babbling about romantic cruises.

"He's going to drive me crazy," groaned Gertrude. But she stood close to the camel, pressing up against his legs for comfort.

Falk was standing next to Elissa, looking very pleased. He had been delighted when Elissa suggested that Maya take the donkey and camel with her as a token of their friendship, though he had briefly considered keeping the camel. As far as he knew, none of the other nobles had one. But in the end, Falk was glad that Elissa had given up the camel as well. Now he would get a proper pet for Elissa—a gentle mare, or a retriever, or perhaps a hawk.

As the carriage pulled slowly away, with Gertrude and Ralph clumping behind it, Elissa waved tearfully. The last words she heard were Gertrude's.

"I'll never forgive you," brayed the donkey accusingly. "You know how much I hate boats."

Falk took Elissa by the arm in an unusual gesture of affection and walked with her through the courtyard. Aldric followed close behind.

"I should begin preparing for the ball, don't you think?" she said sweetly. "Florie says it's going to take all day to dress me."

"Go get dressed," said Falk indulgently as they parted at the stairway leading to the royal chambers.

Elissa took the stairs two at a time.

Falk smiled. "You see?" he said to Aldric. "She's changing."

Oak drove his wagon carefully, for the road was filled with potholes that threatened to shake the wheels from their axles and his bones from their sockets. He had piled the wagon high with straw so the children would not get jostled too much tomorrow, on the way back from the harbor. Fern's husband was leaving today on another long sea voyage, so her family would be moving back in with Oak for a while, at least until Fern's husband returned. Tonight Oak would stay in Fern's little cottage by the bay and help her pack up her things. He clucked sadly. It was always wonderful to have Fern in his house, but he knew how much she missed her husband. She'd be subdued for a day or two after he left. Although perhaps the news of the ball would cheer her up. He'd heard there was to be an announcement this evening. The Princess was going to be engaged.

A figure dressed in the coarse brown cloak of a monk was walking by the side of the track, his hooded head bent and his hands tucked devoutly into his robes. Oak stopped the wagon.

"Care for a ride, Brother?" he called. The monk stopped and turned, but did not speak. It was then that Oak noticed that he had a bag slung over one shoulder. The monk must be one of the King's scribes. They always carried their quills and inks and writing whatnots with them wherever they went.

The monk did not answer, but merely inclined his head in acceptance. Placing his foot on the hub of a wheel, he nimbly climbed up the side of the tall cart, and took a seat beside Oak.

"I'm going down to the harbor," Oak said unnecessarily, for this road led nowhere else. "No doubt ye'll be traveling on the *Northern Star*." The monastery lay to the north. "My daughter's man, Eric, will be sailing with ye, so have no fear, ye'll arrive safely."

The young monk nodded again, but kept quiet. Oak guessed that this must be one of the Silent Ones. The old man continued to talk, however, because it was his habit to chat. Furthermore, with a passenger who had taken a vow of silence, Oak could say whatever he liked, knowing that his words would not be bandied about all through Castlemar.

"It is a pity ye must be leaving before the ball," he said. "Cook says there will feasting for all tonight." Oak's passenger did not even nod at this comment. Perhaps he was one of the ones who did not eat. Just water and dry crusts of bread for them, poor lads.

"Come midnight, the Princess will be betrothed," continued Oak. "And for such an occasion, King Falk will not skimp. Say what ye will, he's a fair man, and just." It never hurt to put in a good word for one's king. However, talk of the Princess put Oak in a thoughtful frame of mind.

"Ay," he sighed. "She's a rare one, that Princess Elissa. I have never seen the likes of her, not since I was a boy and a healer come through these parts from the South. But the Princess has the Touch, I'm telling ye. Nay, I do not lie. Everything she touches thrives. And if ye don't believe me, just look at my daughter's babe! She was weak and crying just a few weeks ago, and now she's as fat as a suckling pig and sleeping like a little lambkin. And my apple orchard! Ye never saw such blossoms! And all she had to do was place her hand on the tired old branches. It was like a miracle." Oak sighed again. The last time he had seen the Princess had been when the young count came to call. He'd sworn there'd been a gleam in her eye when she'd looked at that young man.

"I hope she will be happy," said Oak softly. "It wouldn't do for the Princess to be unhappy, she being such a good, kind lass. Nay, it wouldn't do at all."

To Oak's surprise, the monk put his hand briefly on Oak's arm—just long enough for Oak to feel the light, warm pressure. As they approached the harbor, the old man lapsed into silence. He pulled the wagon alongside the wharf, drawing to a halt when he spotted his excited grandchildren scampering along the docks, whooping with glee, for their grandfather never failed to bring them sweets. Oak descended from his seat slowly. When he turned around to bid the monk a safe journey, the young man had disappeared.

## ❧ 6 ❧

# Sitting Amongst Ghosts

The Western Reach is a land of bare, rocky hills and dry plains, its rugged terrain more often tinged with brown than green. Lacking both the charms of the unspoiled North, and the comforts of the East, the territories of the West are not especially attractive to the outsider. Nevertheless, they were home to Favian. And as he sat upon his mount, surveying the lands of his father's holdings—soon to be his own—Favian felt a certain pride, which he felt obliged to share.

"It may not be pretty," he said to his horse. "But it's Leonne."

He brought the big bay carefully down the stony slope and onto the broad plain that surrounded the manor. A stand of olive trees, their leaves silvered by dust, marked the head of the wide, straight lane that led to the main house. The lane was edged with the vines that produced Leonne's only crop of real significance, which now hung with clusters of green fruit. The wines of Leonne were famous. Vineyards, and an abundance of precious stones, had made Leonne the strongest of the Western holdings. Favian adjusted his sword as he rode toward the manor. Three locks of dark hair dangled from his belt. Although the girls were very silly, theirs had been a romantic gesture, one worthy of a gallant young noble. Yet as he briefly fingered the tresses, he could not help but feel disappointed that they were not russet.

It had been Elissa's face that Favian sought as he rode through Castlemar's gate on Falk's great stallion. He could not help but recall the look of sheer disappointment she had given him when he had shared his news with her beside Oak's cottage. Although Favian's pleasure at regaining his station in life was beyond words, in some ways it had pleased him even more that Elissa had not wanted him to leave.

Now that Favian's mind was traveling along that route, he remembered that there had been something she wanted to tell him. Somehow it had not come up during their conversation. His momentous news had completely overshadowed hers. He now regretted not having heard her out, but he consoled himself with the thought that when he returned, as a legitimate count, with lands and backing to match his title, she would, no doubt, tell him everything. They still might not be considered equals, even after his title had been restored. But as a count, he might be regarded as an acceptable confidant—one worthy of a princess.

He wondered how she was faring. He'd heard her father was holding a ball for her fifteenth birthday. That would be today, the anniversary of the day she had found him nearly perished in the swamp. He would never forget the date, or the embarrassment he'd experienced at being indebted to a commoner. Favian winced as he remembered his chagrin at discovering her true identity. Nevertheless, he was sorry he was going to miss the ball—sorry and somewhat envious. There would be other young men there—nobles, maybe even princes—who would dance with her. And while he himself cut a fine figure on the dance floor, she would never know it. Not that she would care, he reassured himself, for Elissa saw deeply into people. She would never be taken in by any of those high-stepping, smooth-talking, chinless, spineless, pitiful wimps who couldn't even lift a sword, let alone wield it . . . Favian took a deep breath.

*Smoke.*

Quickly, Favian removed his riding gloves and slapped them vigorously against his thigh. They were not badly burned, just a bit singed. He gazed at the blackened palms of his gloves thoughtfully. He would have to control his temper while he was in Leonne. Otherwise he might burn the whole place down.

As the manor came into view, Favian shifted his thoughts away from Elissa's theoretically pathetic but nonetheless potentially threatening suitors and onto other worries. Favian had not sent a messenger to Leonne to announce his arrival but had simply come after receiving his uncle Theo's letter, which meant that no one would be expecting him today. This was what he had intended, of course. It was better to catch his stepmother unprepared. Favian smiled bitterly. When

Sonia had time to think and plan, things never went well for anyone—except for Sonia, of course. He imagined she must know that he would be returning. Or perhaps she didn't know anything of the kind. She might think him dead in the swamps. He would know when he saw her face. Perhaps a brief expression of surprise would flash in her eyes. But no matter how fleeting or well hidden, he would spot it.

The first face he wanted to see was not hers, but Theo's. He needed a chance to speak with his uncle before Sonia discovered he'd arrived. Theo's letter had said only that Favian's half brothers had been killed by their own devices, but he did not explain how. It was unlikely that they had accomplished that deed themselves. His half brothers were brutes, but they were intensely loyal to one another. And their mother, however depraved she might be, was not the kind to kill her own blood. Favian frowned, thinking of eventualities. Sonia was still relatively young. She could remarry; she might even bear another son. He'd have to watch his back.

Favian's preoccupations took him right up to the manor gate. Its double panels, deeply carved with the family crest—two lions rearing up on their hind legs to do battle—were open. Nor was there a guard on duty, which was very lax.

Favian shook his head ruefully. He had to admit that in Leonne, guards would be more useful on the *inside* of the manor, to protect its inhabitants from one another.

He dismounted and looped the reins into a rusty iron hoop set into the wall. There was a trough set close to the ring and a meager pile of hay, which would have to do for now. Soon, a stableboy would notice the horse and attend to it properly. He entered the foyer, which, just as he remembered, was cool and dark, smelling of earth. He looked around at the tapestries, the tiled floor, the heavy carved benches lining the walls. It all looked so familiar, yet somehow strange. Although he had not been gone for very long, everything seemed smaller and shabbier than he remembered. The floor tiles were cracked and uneven, the tapestries threadbare, the benches worn and narrow. He closed his eyes for a moment, trying to remember the way this hall used to look as he ran down it in his carefree youth. But he opened his eyes almost immediately, fleeing from that fantasy. He had never run down these halls, for the floor tiles had always been uneven, and dangerous for small feet; the tapestries had always been moth-eaten, the benches hard and uninviting; and his youth had been anything but carefree.

"Ah, Favian!" a voice cried. "You are here!"

Favian raised his eyes to see the image of his stepmother, Sonia of Arania, descending the stairs to greet him, her slender arms extended, her shapely lips stretched in a cool smile. She was as beautiful as ever—and quite obviously with child.

"My son," she proclaimed with false warmth. "Welcome. We've been expecting you."

Favian followed his stepmother through the eastern wing of the manor, to a small sitting room where she and Theo, as she explained, had been conversing. "Imagine that!" she said, feigning amazement. "We were just talking about you, and here you are!"

Favian hid his disappointment at not being able to talk with Theo in private.

Sonia's face, composed and serene, had not

expressed the tiniest twinge of surprise, much less alarm, at Favian's sudden appearance.

He should have known.

As Favian entered his stepmother's sitting room, his uncle rose and came forward, embracing him tightly with his strong arms. He looked careworn to Favian, but otherwise much the same as when Favian had left—kindly, comfortable, and somewhat melancholy.

"It's good to see you," said Theo simply, though the moisture in his brown eyes spoke volumes. "Very good."

"Will you take some refreshment?" Sonia was smiling, but her invitation, as always, was a command. Favian nodded politely as Sonia signaled a blank-faced servant with her finger. The girl scurried off obediently. "Tell us, what is new in Castlemar?"

Well then, she knew where he had been all along! It seemed no news was "news" to Sonia. Favian thought back. When he had first arrived at Castlemar, he had sent a short message to Theo, deeming it necessary to inform his uncle of his whereabouts, and of his safety. Apparently the letter had fallen into Sonia's hands, or perhaps it had simply been delivered into them. Favian glanced at his uncle before recounting the news of Castlemar. Theo shrugged somewhat apologetically. Inwardly, Favian forgave him. There was no point in trying to hide anything from Sonia.

"The new king, Falk, has been coronated, and fares well," he said. The expressionless serving girl returned, bearing a tray with bread, cheeses, grapes, and a carafe of wine and three cups, which she presented to Favian, eyes fixed on the floor. He offered a cup to Sonia.

"Just a little," she said, patting her round belly. Politely, Theo and Favian waited until she took a sip before drinking from their own cups.

Favian hesitated. He very much wanted to know the details of his half brothers' deaths, but he knew it would be useless to ask. Sonia would never reveal any more information than suited her, which was always as little as possible. He decided to give her his condolences instead.

"I would like to express my deepest sympathies over the deaths of your sons," he said formally.

"They were your brothers as well," she reminded him, dabbing at the corner of her eyes with a bit of lace. With her black veil and porcelain skin, she looked the very picture of delicate bereavement.

"Yes," said Favian. Technically they were considered his brothers, though he had never addressed them as such—nor had he wanted to, any more than he would ever concede to calling Sonia "Mother."

"You must call me 'Mother' now," she said, as if reading his thoughts. "For you are the only heir left. That is, until my son is born."

Favian turned his eyes to Theo, who up until this time had not spoken a word. Looking away, Theo frowned and cleared his throat.

"I am afraid I forgot to mention in my letter that the Countess had remarried," he mumbled through his mustache. Sonia cast him a meaningful look. Apparently the omission had not been accidental; just one of Sonia's little ploys to catch Favian off guard.

"You didn't know?" she asked Favian innocently. "Why, Theo, how could you have forgotten such a thing? Julian and I were married last year," she continued. "You remember Julian, don't you? Your father's cousin?"

*Ensuring the proper bloodline,* thought Favian.

He nodded, mentally conjuring up the moist, pale face of his sickly cousin. Julian was the ideal mate for Sonia: weak, witless, and easily led. Controlling him would be effortless.

"I am sorry Julian could not be here to greet you himself," said Sonia. "But he had to attend to some business."

With this rather transparent lie, there remained not a shred of doubt in Favian's mind that Sonia was plotting something. Julian, as everyone knew, never had anything to attend to. She had undoubtedly sent her bumbling husband off to get him safely out from underfoot. Sonia preferred to do her dirty work unobserved. Her next statement confirmed Favian's worst suspicions.

"More's the pity that Theo has to leave as well. So it will be just you and me this evening," she said. "We have so much to talk about." Her smile was dangerously bright.

"We do indeed," Favian replied cautiously. "But I am very tired. Might I not sup alone tonight?"

Sonia consented graciously. "Naturally. You must be weary after your travels. But do come join me for a glass of wine before you go to bed, won't you?"

"Of course," said Favian. What else could he say?

"We dine at eight. I will send a servant to fetch you when I am ready," she said, offering her hand for Favian to kiss. As always, she wore a bulky ring with her family crest engraved upon it. The thought occurred to him that the ring was far too large for her slender fingers. He took her hand in his own and bent his head, but his lips did not touch the cool, dry skin.

"Until then," he said.

Claiming that he needed to check on his horse, Favian declined to follow the house servant to his quarters. Although there was really no need for him to attend to the bay; the stablehands would have already seen to it that his mount was watered, fed, and brushed down—as indeed they had. But this was the one place he might find Theo, if only because they both knew they would be assured of a private conversation in the stalls. The manor servants—Sonia's spies, every one of them—did not like to leave the comforts of the main house. True to his expectations, Theo was waiting for him.

"My dear boy!" Theo exclaimed. "I was so happy to hear that you were still alive!"

"So you knew what Sonia had planned for me?" asked Favian, sitting down heavily on a bale of hay.

Theo sighed and sat next to him. "I suspected. When you left, I sent a small party after you," he said. "Just in case Sonia decided to take matters into her own hands. But they lost your trail in Al-hamazar. When they returned without you, I feared the worst."

"As you can see, they did not succeed," said Favian, "though they tried. I was accosted in Al-hamazar and left to die in the swamps." He didn't tell Theo about his rescue or about Elissa, much as he would have liked to. One had to take pre-cautions. Until he knew exactly what Sonia had up her sleeve, he did not want to jeopardize his uncle by giving him too much information. It was best that he remain ignorant.

"I must be off," said Theo suddenly, too loudly. A stablehand had appeared, leading a white horse by a bridle. The boy eyed both Theo and Favian attentively as they walked into the courtyard. Apparently, Sonia's web of spies now included

the stableboys. Theo embraced Favian affection-
ately, kissing him soundly on both cheeks, as was
the custom between kin; and holding him close,
he whispered a few fond words of farewell in Favian's ear. Then he mounted his horse and rode
out of the courtyard toward the west. Theo had
several estates in the west, as Favian recalled.

Favian made his way slowly back to the house,
contemplating his uncle's parting words.

"Accept nothing from her hand," he had
whispered.


Favian dressed carefully. He wanted to look his
best tonight, just in case these were the last
clothes he would be seen in, so he donned the elegant black breeches and the black silk shirt
Falk's tailors had stitched for him. He regarded
his image in the mirror. Favian thought he looked
especially handsome in black, which meant he always looked his finest at funerals—though, in
this particular instance, he hoped the one he next
attended would not be his own. Favian always
felt energized before a battle.

By the time a servant knocked at his door, he
was prepared for anything.

He rose and, at the last moment, remembered to unbuckle his sword. It would be rude to wear a weapon in his stepmother's apartments. He sighed as he dropped his sword on the bed. Rude, but perhaps advisable.

He followed the faceless servant down the hall to Sonia's private chambers. The servant knocked softly, and another equally expressionless servant opened the door. Did none of them smile? Favian thought not. Sonia treated all her servants wretchedly and expected complete unquestioning devotion in return—which, against all reason, she got.

Sonia was sitting in a high-backed chair next to a low carved table. She had removed her veil for the occasion to reveal her wealth of glossy golden hair. It shone brightly in the flickering firelight, undimmed, Favian noted, by the passage of the years. If anything, mature womanhood had heightened Sonia's beauty and turned it into something more powerful, more dangerous. She gestured toward a chair set at a slight angle to hers.

*My father sat in this very chair,* thought Favian

as he seated himself. The unbidden memory of his father sitting here disturbed him. Even more disconcerting was the knowledge that the other chair, the one that supported Sonia, had been his mother's. They had sat facing one another in these chairs: his father and his mother, his father and Sonia. Favian was suddenly overcome with the feeling that he was sitting amongst ghosts. The skin on the back of his neck prickled. Sonia beckoned a servant. Was it the same one who had served them earlier? Favian couldn't tell. They all looked so much alike.

"My special wine," ordered Sonia.

The servant left the room silently.

"Now," said Sonia, tilting her perfect face up at him. "You must tell me everything." Sonia's voice never failed to startle him. It was surprisingly deep, contrasting sharply with her delicate features. Favian imagined that his father had been utterly deceived by Sonia's fragile, doll-like beauty, equating it with a corresponding fragility of spirit. Ultimately, that had been his father's greatest mistake.

"I really have very little to tell," said Favian,

stalling. He was reluctant to talk about Castlemar—especially as concerned Elissa. Favian was
afraid he would be unable to keep the warmth
from his voice. Sonia would be sure to take ad-
vantage of that weakness. "It seems that more
significant events have occurred here."

Sonia dropped her head sadly. "Ah," she sighed
mournfully. "My poor lambs. Such dear, sweet
boys. I suppose Theo has told you all about it."

"Why, no. He hasn't," said Favian innocently,
knowing that Sonia would not have allowed Theo
to divulge any details.

"It was such a terrible tragedy," she said. "I
fear I will never recover."

Favian faced his stepmother as she spoke and
looked into her eyes. They were bright blue—the
color of cornflowers—and completely dry.

"The two of them were working together on
an invention, something Avaro had thought up.
You know how he always took the lead. There
was . . . an accident. An explosion."

Favian could not imagine the "boys" doing
anything constructive together, much less working on an invention. They had never shown any

118

sign of creativity while he had known them, unless one wanted to include ingenious methods of torturing small animals. Favian was relieved, for the world's sake, that they had not grown to adulthood. The twins were barely fifteen when they died. But Avaro's "guidance" had already led them both to unspeakable acts of cruelty.

"What kind of invention was it?" asked Favian, his curiosity aroused.

"Oh, some kind of weapon," said Sonia vaguely. "You know I understand nothing of machines." Favian agreed with Sonia on this point. The engineering of people, not things, was her strong point. "Unfortunately, they are dead now, so we will never know what great accomplishment they were about to achieve."

Favian felt a familiar sensation in his palms. How odd. Normally, he only felt them tingle when he was close to fire. Yet they had tingled as Sonia spoke. He looked down at his hands thoughtfully.

"Ah," Sonia announced. "Here is the wine." A young serving girl had brought a crystal carafe and two wine goblets, which she set on the small table beside Sonia. By the time Favian looked up, the girl had disappeared. Sonia's servants had a knack for quick escapes, and invisibility.

"You must drink with me," she said, "to celebrate your return." She twisted around in her chair to pour the wine into the goblets. He heard the tinkling of the liquid, though Sonia's back hid her hands from him. Then she turned to him and handed Favian a goblet, her eyes fixed upon his face.

"Drink," she commanded.

Favian looked at the goblet she held out to him. It was solid gold, encrusted with a ring of gemstones where the narrow bowl met the long, elegant stem, a stem that Sonia now encased in her slim, elegant fingers. There were two such vessels. The pair had been a gift to the newlyweds on his father's marriage to Sonia, from her mother, he believed. He had seen Sonia offer this goblet to his father on many occasions, had heard her command him to drink.

"Let us make a toast," Favian suggested as he took the goblet. "To Leonne, and to promises kept."

Sonia looked slightly puzzled, but touched

her goblet to his nevertheless. "To Leonne," she said, lifting her goblet to her lips just as Favian lifted his. The wine smelled sweet. Favian preferred his wine dry.

They were interrupted by a sudden sharp rap at the door.

"Who can that be?" cried Sonia. "I told them I was not to be disturbed." She placed her goblet on the table and strode to the door in a fury, jerking it open with both hands.

"Theo!" she exclaimed. "What are you doing here?"

"I am so sorry to intrude," said Theo. "My horse threw a shoe, and I had to return to have him reshod. It was slow going, but I thought it better to return than to risk having the beast go lame on the long journey."

"Indeed!" said Favian. "A good horse must not be wasted." Although Favian was nodding his approval, he cast a brief quizzical glance at Theo, knowing that his uncle never did his horses the indignity of shoeing them. Theo smiled innocently.

Sonia hesitated the merest fraction of a second before inviting Theo to take some wine with them. She clapped her hands, and a servant appeared.

"Another cup," she ordered. "We were just about to toast," she explained to Theo. "Perhaps you will join us?"

"I would love to," answered Theo. The servant presented him with a cup on a tray. "Don't trouble yourself," he said, reaching for the carafe. "I'll pour it myself."

Favian held up his goblet. Sonia and Theo followed suit. "To Leonne!" they said.

They brought their wine to their lips and drank deeply to Leonne—even Sonia, who had previously said she'd only wanted a little. Then they sat in silence.

Sonia yawned.

"It seems I am suddenly weary," she said. "Perhaps we shall resume our little talk tomorrow."

Theo rose immediately. "Many pardons," he said. "The Countess needs her rest." He nodded to Favian, and they made their exit together.

As they walked down the dim corridor, Theo leaned close. "You did pour your own wine, didn't

you?" he asked in a low voice. Theo's thick eyebrows were knit together in concern.

"No," replied Favian. "I didn't—"

"Gods, man!" cried Theo, clutching Favian by
the arm. "We must get you to a healer! Now!"

Suddenly a shrill, piercing scream echoed
down the long, dark hall.

"I switched goblets," said Favian.

# 7

## Stowaway

Oak had no idea why he had been called to the castle. When he'd returned to the cottage, his wagon loaded high with sweet hay and Fern's small, bouncing children, two soldiers were waiting for him. "The King wishes to speak with you. Come!" they had ordered in loud voices, as if they had never drunk his cider or sat in the shade of his orchards on a hot summer's day. In spite of the soldiers and the strangeness of being called to see the King, Oak was not alarmed, and so he bade goodbye to Fern and her tumbling children with an easy heart. King Falk had a reputation for fairness, which meant that he inspired a feeling of security, if not always love, in his subjects. In all truth, Oak, who was a simple man, thought he had been summoned because the orchards were exceptionally beautiful this spring. He believed that everyone shared his delight in growing things. Oak was too close to the earth to think otherwise.

The two guards uncrossed their staffs as Oak and the soldiers approached the audience chamber. They grasped the iron rings that had been bolted into the great double doors and pulled them open, revealing a high-ceilinged room. Oak entered alone. The room was occupied only by the King and a tall, serious-looking man, Aldric. Oak recognized him as Falk's former Captain of the Guard. He now held a position that Oak could not name, but knew to be of great importance. The fact that Aldric was here as well meant that this must be a matter of significance. Oak drew himself up with pride. No doubt the King wanted to hear of Elissa's important contribution to the apple harvest. Just as crops need steady rain, a man's pride in his children must be continually fed.

Aldric regarded the man who approached the throne with careful scrutiny.

"Your Highness," said Oak, bowing before the King.

"Oak," Falk said sternly. "Do you know why you have been called before us today?"

Oak looked directly at the King. The monarch looked careworn, as though he had not slept the night before.

"The orchards, Your Majesty?" Oak held his hands straight down at his sides. His fingernails, like those of any man who works close to the earth, were dirty.

Falk turned blank eyes upon Oak.

"The blooms are so thick this spring, the harvest will be plentiful," continued Oak. "Even the pears are doing uncommon well . . . in spite of the drought." The more Oak described the bounty of the orchards, the more the King frowned.

The King glanced at Aldric. Oak could not read the look that passed between them, but somehow he knew that it did not bode well for him. Perhaps the King was not pleased with his fruit trees after all. A pity.

"I have heard that you went down to the harbor yesterday," said Falk.

"Yes, indeed I did, sire," said Oak warmly. He was happy to speak about his trip to the sea, though he did not know why the King should take an interest in it. Nevertheless, it was a King's right to ask, and Oak's duty to answer. "I went to fetch my daughter Fern and her wee babes. They always stay with me when her husband, Eric . . . oh, he's a fine lad . . . when Eric puts out to sea."

"And did anyone accompany you on that trip?" asked the King. His face had taken on a fixed expression, as if these questions were a mere formality, their answers already being known to him.

"No, not properly speaking," said Oak carefully. "I took no fares, nor hauled any goods. Except I did give a ride to a young monk who was walking by the side of the road."

"Did you speak of anything?" Falk's tone was even, but his eyes were dark and unblinking.

Oak managed to look simultaneously embarrassed and proud. "Aye," he said, lapsing into dialect. "I spake of the orchards, and my garden—and of the Princess. The Brother spake naught at all, he being one of the Silent Ones."

Falk did not respond immediately, but merely

focused his intent gaze upon the man who stood before him. He spoke slowly. "Exactly what did you say?"

"Well, sire," began the old man. "The Princess came to visit me and Fern. Fern's new babe had a powerful colic, you see, and the Princess recommended a tea . . ."

Oak faltered. The King was scowling at him so fiercely, he had completely lost his train of thought. It suddenly occurred to Oak that it was not proper for a princess to be visiting a gardener. Perhaps there were laws against it. Punishments . . .

"Go on!" said Falk impatiently.

"Fern wanted to thank her," finished Oak. The truth somehow sounded weak to his own ears.

"Is that all you wanted?" The King's eyes bored into Oak's very soul. Oak trembled. He did not understand why the King looked so angry.

"It seemed the proper thing to do," Oak stammered. "She had already made the apple trees to bloom so lovely. And then, when she cured the baby, I knew she had the Touch. So I asked her to lay her hands on the saplings, and ye should see them now, sire, growing so straight and strong.

The Touch is a rare thing. That is why I asked her, sire. Was it wrong of me?" Oak stopped speaking, his lips frozen with distress. The King continued to look at him but said nothing, which only increased Oak's anxiety. The old man wished to appease his King, to say something that would erase that incredulous look from his lord's face, a look that said that he did not believe a word Oak had said. But it seemed everything that came out of Oak's mouth simply made matters worse.

Falk finally turned to Aldric. "What, in all the gods' names, is this man talking about?"

Aldric addressed Oak for the first time, taking the reins of the interrogation from the hands of his exasperated lord. "You are saying that the reason you invited Princess Elissa to your hut was to touch your trees?"

"Yes, sir," said Oak humbly, relieved to the point of tears that someone understood. "She has the Healing Touch," he said again, as though that explained everything. To Oak's mind, it did.

Oak looked at the King as he spoke, hoping for comprehension, but the monarch merely looked perplexed, and frustrated.

"And the monk? What did he look like?" continued Aldric patiently.

Oak was eager to change the topic, away from trees and the King's daughter, although, on the subject of the monk, he had very little to offer. "I don't rightly know," he answered honestly. "He kept his hood drawn down over his face the whole time. A young lad, I think. But I never got a proper look at him, nor even had a chance to say a fare-thee-well. When I got to the harbor, he just disappeared."

The King shot Aldric a quick glance and nodded. Aldric waved toward the door, signifying that the audience was over. Oak felt as if he had escaped from harm's way, though the fact that he could not name the danger he had faced, or justify it, caused him to feel obscurely wronged. The gardener was too mild and humble a man to recognize this feeling in himself. Nevertheless, when the King raised his hand to dismiss Oak, the old man found himself speaking.

"She's a fine lass, your daughter," he said quietly. "One to make any man proud." Then he bowed, turned his back to the King, and walked from the room, apparently ignorant of the fact that a commoner never turns his back on a king. The King might have noticed this breach of etiquette had his thoughts not been elsewhere.

Falk spoke first. "If there is a plot, I will know of it." He struck his hand angrily against the arm of the throne. "I will pry it out of this man, alone or with assistance. Castlemar has a fully equipped dungeon, which I am more than willing to throw this man into if he continues to withhold information."

Aldric shook his head. "He knows nothing," he said. "Oak has been in service for more years than I can remember. He is a simple soul, my lord, as you can see."

Falk slumped in his throne wearily. "You are right," said the King. "Although I have no idea what that 'touching' thing was all about."

"It's just a peasant belief," said Aldric. "A superstition. Nothing of importance." He waited for Falk to speak.

Falk replayed the interview with Oak in his mind. At this point even Falk had to abandon the theory that Elissa had been abducted. He and Aldric had personally questioned everyone who had left the castle for any reason within the past twenty-four hours, and there was simply no evidence. Nor would there have been any motivation for a kidnapping, with no ongoing wars or upcoming invasions. Falk sighed.

"Then she must have run away," he said. He made the admission with an equal measure of resignation and shame. An abduction would at least have given Falk an enemy to fight. A way to save face.

"I do believe she has," said Aldric. "All the highways, forests, and farms have been searched within a thirty-mile radius, to no avail. And one of the monks' hoods is indeed missing from the library. I think it would be reasonable, given what Oak has reported, to assume that she boarded a ship."

"There were two ships in the harbor yesterday," said Falk. "The *Northern Star* and the *Southern Cross*."

"It is likely that she boarded the *Southern Cross*," said Aldric. "The Princess was very fond of Maya," he added. "Very fond."

Falk realized that Aldric was making a point, in his own understated way.

"Come out with it," Falk said. He was willing

to face the music, even if the tune was not to his liking.

"I have heard it said that if a man wishes to see what he will become, he has only to look at his father," said Aldric circuitously.

Falk knuckled his brow, trying to free his thoughts from the confines of his hard, hard head. "And if a man wishes to see his father, he has only to look into a mirror. I know, Aldric, I know. You've said it before. But my father was a despot, a tyrant. He planned to have my wife murdered, and if he had been able to find Elissa, he probably would have killed her as well! I am not the man he was, not even remotely." He looked up, his eyes pleading. "You of all people should see that. I would never harm Elissa. I love her."

"I'd be willing to wager my post as Chief Advisor that you have never said those words to her," said Aldric. He knew he was being hard on Falk. But the lesson must finally be driven home now, while Falk was open to it, or there would be endless flights, endless strife, and endless disruption in Castlemar.

Falk did not, indeed could not, answer Aldric.

He ordered a ship, a light, swift vessel, to follow and overtake the *Southern Cross*. Then he returned to his chambers to spend the remainder of the day alone with his mirror.

At first Elissa could hardly believe her wonderful luck. If old Oak had not come along at precisely the right moment, the ship would have left without her. Her luck continued when she reached the wharf, where she found a stack of large baskets that were to be loaded onto the ship. She opened one to find a dozen beady eyes looking up at her morosely.

"Are we there yet?" the hens asked all at once.

"You're not going anywhere," whispered Elissa. "Now hop out and run away as quickly as you can."

"Oh, goody!" clucked the hens. "We didn't want to go on this cruise anyway. We've heard the food is terrible and the service is even worse. And let me tell you, sitting on a clutch of eggs while your nest goes up and down and up and down is enough to wear your tail feathers off."

"Out!" commanded Elissa. The hens scattered. Then, rapidly, while no one was looking, she dumped the straw out of the basket and climbed in, closing the lid as firmly as she could behind her. It was a tight squeeze, but if she lay on her side and drew her knees up to her chest, she just fit. She hoped she wouldn't have to stay in that position for long. The basket smelled rankly of chickens. She heard voices. Elissa clutched her bag against her chest and held her breath as she was hoisted up and carried away.

"That one goes on top," she heard a man say. She felt herself being swung upward and placed onto a boat. She could see the occasional glimmer of water through the tiny cracks in the wicker as they rocked along. Then she felt the basket being lifted steadily upward and finally hoisted onto a strong shoulder.

"Awfully heavy for chickens," she heard the man grumble as the basket was jounced down a flight of steps. He dropped the basket with a thud. "Must be a calf or something."

There was silence, and then darkness as the hatch closed. Elissa remained curled in a fetal position, not daring to move until she heard the creaking of the ship's anchor being raised.

*We're under way!* she thought. *I've done it!* She

couldn't wait to get out of the confines of the basket and find Maya. But it probably would be best to remain hidden for a little while longer, until the ship was far out to sea and could not possibly return to Castlemar's harbor.

In spite of her happiness at having escaped from the castle, Elissa felt a small qualm about running away. It was a cowardly act—certainly not one befitting a princess, even though she had never really thought of herself as one. In her own eyes, Elissa was not worthy of that title. Princesses were born, not made. And all her father's attempts to transform her into one had merely made her feel inadequate. In spite of that knowledge, she felt somewhat diminished, even ashamed. For all that she resented her father's machinations, she had held on to the hope that one day she would deserve his respect. Hiding in a chicken basket somehow did not seem like anything to be proud of, even if it would eventually lead to her freedom.

It was horribly uncomfortable in the small space allotted for the hens. Elissa tried to ease her cramped legs and found she could not. Her knees were in agony. She absolutely had to straighten them out. It was not likely that anyone would be coming down into the hold this early in the trip, so surely she could risk a little stretch. Elissa opened the lid of the basket cautiously. It was very dark in the hold, and smelly. Elissa wrinkled up her nose at the pungent odors of manure and rotted straw. *They really ought to clean this place out*, she thought as she gratefully straightened her legs. *Animals don't like being dirty any more than we do.* Oh, it felt so good to stretch. Even better would be to walk. Elissa lowered herself out of the basket and gingerly placed her feet on the sticky floor. Almost immediately she heard the sound of voices. She barely had enough time to get back into the basket before the hatch was thrown open.

"Get one of the fat ones," she heard. "The Captain is entertaining a *lady* tonight." There was a short burst of raucous laughter and the sound of footsteps. A moment later, the lid of the basket was thrown open and Elissa found herself looking up into a grubby, and completely astonished, face.

"Hello," she said.

"You don't look much like a chicken," replied the man. He reached in and roughly pulled Elissa out by her arm.

"If I could just have a word with your captain," she said as he led her up the steps.

"Don't worry, you'll have *one*," said the man grimly. "And he'll have exactly three words for you."

They walked across the deck, evoking stares from the other deckhands. Elissa was pleased to see that the shore was already very distant. In fact, she could hardly see it. They entered the Captain's quarters.

"What have we here?" asked the Captain coldly. He was a hard-looking man with a large, bony nose and a small, tight mouth.

"Stowaway, sir," replied the deckhand. "I found her in with the livestock."

The Captain rose from his desk and walked over to where Elissa, still being held tightly by the deckhand, was standing. The Captain gestured for the sailor to release her arm.

"Well, what have you to say for yourself?" asked the Captain. From the tone of his voice, it did not sound as if the Captain was expecting a reply. Nonetheless, Elissa tried to answer.

"I am Elissa," she said. As she spoke, she realized that her coarse brown cloak would not help identify her. "Princess Elissa, and I . . ."

Elissa never finished her proclamation, for the Captain and the sailor had both begun to laugh uproariously. "Take her up and dump her," said the Captain after he'd regained his composure.

*Dump?* Elissa did not know quite what the Captain meant, but it didn't sound good. "If you'll only listen," she said. "I can explain."

"Quiet!" the Captain barked. "Get Eric." One of the sailors who had followed behind them ran off. Within moments, an immense blond sailor appeared. *"Toss her overboard!"* ordered the Captain.

Elissa was instantly grabbed and hoisted right off her feet.

"I am the Princess!" she cried as she was hauled out of the room. "Ask Maya; she'll tell you."

The Captain chuckled. "Who in blazes is Maya?"

"My friend Maya!" cried Elissa. "She's on your ship—"

"You are completely mad," said the Captain,

enunciating his words slowly. "But mad or sane, it makes no difference. Stowaways get tossed. It is the rule of the sea whether I or anybody else likes it or not. And now, it's time for your bath—*Your Highness*." He ignored her protests as the huge sailor bore her away.

"Close that door," he said to the deckhand.

Elissa could not believe her ears. They were going to throw her into the middle of the ocean!

"You have to listen to me!" she cried to the sailor. But her voice was muffled by his wool jacket. The man was carrying her over his broad left shoulder like a sack of potatoes. One of his powerful arms grasped her feet so she could not kick; the other was clamped tightly about her waist.

"Stowaways get tossed," he said. "Cap'n says so."

The sailor made his way to the side of the boat, through the crowd of sailors who had stopped working for a moment to watch the tossing. When he reached the railing, he adjusted Elissa so that he was cradling her in his arms, like a fussy infant who needed to be rocked to sleep. She looked up into the sailor's face. His blue eyes looked sad. He began to swing Elissa back, in preparation for heaving her over the side. She kicked her legs uselessly and began to utter her final frantic protest, "Don't—" Then she remembered.

*"Eric!"* she cried. "You're Fern's husband!" The huge man stopped in mid-swing.

"Aye," he said slowly. "I'm Fern's man."

"I cured your baby," Elissa said desperately. "She was colicky, and I recommended the tea."

Eric held Elissa in his arms and looked down at her. Fern had told him that the baby never stopped crying, and how the tea had calmed her. She'd also told him about the green-eyed princess who had cured the infant. The sailor looked into Elissa's eyes for a long while. Then he set her gently on the deck.

"What is going on here?" The Captain had emerged from his quarters and was striding toward them. "I gave an order!"

"Captain—" Eric began to speak, but he halted as he saw a movement out of the corner of his eye. It was the passenger, and she was making her way quickly toward them.

"Elissa!" she cried. "What are you doing here?"

The Captain turned to face his guest. "You know this girl?"

"Yes, of course I do," she said. Coming forward through the crowd, the Windsinger took Elissa's trembling hands in her own pale fingers and turned to face the Captain with her ever-changing opal eyes, her hair fluffing about her head in a soft white halo. "She is the Princess of Castlemar."

## ⤞ 8 ⤝

# The Truth

The day that Favian was to be instated as Count of Leonne was delayed a week in order to allow the customary mourning period for the former countess, Sonia of Arania. Personally, Favian thought an hour or two would have been sufficient—perhaps not even that long. Although he realized that his sentiments could be interpreted as callous, he knew they were shared, for the servants, even dressed for a funeral, men in black jackets and women in mourning veils, looked happier than he had ever seen them. He couldn't, in fact, recall a time when they had seemed more alive. During his childhood, when the maids lined up each morning for Sonia's daily instructions, they had always reminded him of a row of bricks—dull, hard, and all precisely the same. Now, much to his amazement, their faces seemed to bloom with features that smiled, greeted him, showed character and personality. Perhaps their transformation should not come as such a surprise. Sonia had ruled Leonne with a heart made of stone and an iron fist, both of which the servants had often felt.

Nevertheless, Favian felt a pang of remorse as they carried her on a flower-strewn bier to the family crypt. Even in death she was beautiful. Julian, his pale face puffy with grief, wept piteously as they laid her beside her former husband and Favian's father, Count Beltran.

"My poor baby," sobbed Julian. Favian had the distinct feeling that the man was not referring to his wife, but to their unborn child. Julian was graying at the temples, but as yet had no children. Although Favian felt little guilt over Sonia's death, he held himself deeply responsible for leaving Julian without an heir.

"You really didn't have much of a choice," said Theo consolingly. They were sitting together in Favian's chambers, sharing a glass of burgundy.

"You could not have known the wine would be fatal."

"Why did she do it?" mused Favian. "I know I was a threat to her, but such a blatant and open attempt at murder . . ."

"She was desperate," Theo said. "You were her last real obstacle to total power. As Countess, she would have ruled in her child's place for many years, and then, as she did with the twins, she would have retained control even after Julian's child came of age." Theo pulled at his mustache thoughtfully. "I believe she did not intend to kill you outright, though."

"How not?" asked Favian. "There was enough poison in that goblet to kill her almost immediately."

"Yes," agreed Theo. "But remember, Sonia was a very small woman. There was probably not enough poison in your wine to kill *you* immediately. I think her intent was to make you quite ill and keep you that way, as she did your father."

Favian stared at Theo, aghast. "You mean she poisoned my father?"

Theo looked uncomfortable. He hesitated

before speaking. "I *suspect* that she did. Of course, there was no proof." Indeed, Theo had strongly suspected her of poisoning Beltran, as they all had. Yet he had done nothing. None of them had done anything. Not one single noble or any of the servants had dared, lest they suffer the same fate.

Favian remembered the stomach pains and the retching. His father's white, sweating face and shaking hands; the endless bloodlettings. Count Beltran had died a miserable death, but it was one that Favian felt he had richly deserved.

"He had it coming to him," said Favian coldly. "It was his punishment for killing my mother."

Theo looked at Favian, astounded. "Do you really think your father murdered your mother— his own wife?" he asked.

"Yes," replied Favian, calmly. "I always have."

Theo looked at Favian's face. He was young, not quite twenty. No lines marked the smooth contours of his cheeks and brow. Yet Theo saw traces around Favian's eyes and mouth of a deep-seated, tightly held anger.

"Your father did not kill Rowenna," said Theo firmly. "It was an accident."

"That is precisely what *he* claimed!" cried

Favian, suddenly incensed. "But it is not true. My father married Sonia less than a month after my mother died. He was besotted! He killed my mother to get her out of the way!"

Theo's mustache drooped sadly around his mouth. "Ah, Favian," he said sadly. "To have lived with such a belief all this time. Your father was a bit of a brute, it is true, but he was no murderer. You see, dear boy, I witnessed the accident myself. Her horse balked when a snake crossed her path, and she was thrown into a tree. Her neck was broken instantly. I know, Favian, because I was there. I tried to revive her, but she died in my arms. Your father wept, Favian. I remember it well." Theo remembered that day all too clearly, as much as he would like to forget it—Rowenna's strange cry; the sickening thump as she hit the tree trunk; the narrow red ribbon slithering through the tall grass; and, most terrible of all, the smile that curved her lips even as his tears fell upon them.

Favian was gazing numbly at his uncle. "All these years," he whispered. "And I was wrong."

"Don't blame yourself." Theo laid his hand on Favian's shoulder. There was kindness in his touch.

"You were only a child, and you loved her very much. You were so hurt, so angry; you had to blame someone. And your father was not gentle with you. It must have appeared to you that he had simply traded one wife for another."

Favian leaned forward and lowered his head onto his arms. Theo understood that his nephew wished to be alone.

"I will come back in an hour," said Theo. He stood up, but to his surprise, Favian reached out and stopped him.

"Take this," he said, placing a small object into Theo's hand. "Here is your proof."

Theo looked down at the object Favian had given him. It was Sonia's family ring. He examined it carefully, found the little spring mechanism that opened the top, revealing a tiny hollow chamber. Theo sniffed cautiously at the traces of white powder that remained within it.

"If you prefer, you need not show it to anyone else," said Favian wearily. "You all know the truth anyway."

Favian watched as Theo's expression changed from horror to shame. Favian had always considered Theo a good, honorable man. And Theo had done his best to protect his nephew. But being good-hearted is never enough.

"The ruthless do not respect the good, nor do they obey rules of honor," Favian said.

Theo gripped Sonia's ring in his hand, as if to engrave that lesson upon his palm.

After her rescue from imminent drowning, Elissa was bundled up and taken to the Captain's quarters, whereupon accepting his profuse apologies, she was fed a hot meal and offered his own bed. Aesha stayed with Elissa, quietly watching and waiting.

Elissa was obviously quite upset. The air around her was moving in small, agitated eddies, quite unlike the slow circular flow of air that usually surrounded Elissa. Aesha wanted to do something for Elissa, to say some words that would soothe her, but, having kept herself so isolated at Castlemar, she did not quite understand the nature of Elissa's distress.

"I'm on the wrong ship," Elissa said again. She had said this several times already. Up until now, Aesha had merely nodded and waited patiently. But Elissa had not explained.

"Which is the right ship?" Aesha inquired hesitantly.

"The *Southern Cross*," said Elissa. "The ship that Maya and Gertrude are on. I was supposed to go home with Maya, to her island."

"Whatever for?" asked Aesha. "Isn't your home in Castlemar, with your father?"

"No, Aesha," said Elissa, sighing deeply. "I have no home." It was true. Her father simply meant to marry her off to the highest bidder. And she couldn't very well go back to High Crossing—not now. Falk would expect that and would track her down.

"My father was going to announce my engagement to one of his cousins—Lord Gavin—at the ball," she explained.

"And you were trying to escape the marriage?" asked Aesha.

"Yes," said Elissa. "No. I mean, that isn't all. You see, he was trying to separate me from my friends, from you and Favian and Maya . . . and even Gertrude . . . so that I would do as he wished. I didn't run away just because he wanted me to marry, but because he tried to take away everything that mattered to me . . . behind my back. It wasn't just the Duke; I was escaping from my father." Elissa struggled to put her feelings—both the long-standing resentments and the newly discovered ones—into words. "I felt trapped."

The Windsinger looked thoughtful. "Ah," whispered Aesha. "I see. He wanted to lock you in a cage—a lovely cage filled with comforts and beauty, but from which you could never escape, for your friends would all be too far away to unlock the door."

Elissa was glad that Aesha understood, even if her interpretation of events was somewhat odd. It made Elissa feel so much better to talk to the Windsinger.

Aesha observed the eddies of air as, once again, they began to flow smoothly around Elissa. She smiled.

"You will find your home," she said. "Everything will be all right."

The *Northern Star* set anchor at Northport several days later, just before sunset. Northport was a dingy, makeshift little town consisting of no more than a dozen rickety buildings, all of which, to varying degrees, seemed to be leaning away

151

from the sea. Elissa thought that years of being buffeted by the chill North Sea winds had perhaps made the houses want to escape inland. But, being moored to the earth by their foundations, they could do no more than lean and twist away from the wind that battered at their sides. It seemed that the sea surrounding Northport was perpetually on the verge of a full-blown tempest. Wind was, in fact, the principal characteristic of the Far North, as Aesha informed her when they disembarked. The Captain himself escorted them to Northport's only inn, an establishment that boasted a single guest room, into which the Captain personally installed them. Ever since Elissa's close encounter with the watery depths, the Captain had been especially deferential toward her, though he still looked as though he had just eaten a lemon whenever he spoke to her.

"We'll be berthed here for a week to take on cargo," he said. "Then we'll take you back to Castlemar."

Elissa sighed. She did not want to return. But she certainly could not stay here. She sat on her hard mattress, gazing out of the room's single window. It was small, and dirty, and half obscured by the bed, but if she ducked her head just so, she could see the magnificent white-capped peaks of the Great Circle. Looking at them, she wondered how anyone could live in such a desolate place. She turned to Aesha, who was sitting on the bed opposite Elissa, feeding her little bird, Sweetheart.

Aesha mystified Elissa. For weeks, if not months, she had seemed to exist in quite another world, and now she was completely in tune with her surroundings. As Elissa watched Aesha offering Sweetheart tiny scraps of food, which the bird took up delicately in his little beak, she wondered what it was that Aesha saw with those eerie eyes of hers. Even when she appeared to be looking right at people, it rather seemed to Elissa that she was looking through or around them.

"Where do you put Sweetheart when he is not on your shoulder?" asked Elissa curiously. Most of the time the bird kept close to Aesha's ear, but at times he disappeared.

"I kept the cage Billy gave me," replied Aesha. "So that Sweetheart would have a place to sleep. But I took the door off, so he can get out anytime. How can you tell Sweetheart is male? I did not know that."

Aesha had noticed that Elissa had said "he." Elissa wondered what else Aesha had noticed.

"I know a lot about animals," said Elissa easily. "I grew up among farmers." It was a true enough statement, although, in this case, she had known Sweetheart was a male because of her Gift.

Aesha gazed at the space around Elissa.

"That is not completely true," said Aesha quietly. "You know because of something else."

Elissa gave Aesha a long, speculative look. "How did you find out?" she asked finally. "Did Maya tell you?" Even as she asked the question, Elissa knew that Maya hadn't said a word.

Once again Aesha looked toward Elissa, but not at her. "No one needed to tell me," she said quietly. She was silent for such a long time that Elissa thought the Windsinger must have decided not to explain. Then, unexpectedly, she extended her hands toward Elissa, and, in a strange, almost dancelike movement, undulated her fingers and palms, raising and lowering her hands, then swirling them downward. She seemed to be feeling something soft and flowing, like water or silk, but there was nothing but empty space around Elissa. Nothing but air.

Enlightenment spread across Elissa's face. "Ah!" she cried. "You can see the air!"

Aesha nodded. She then raised her eyebrows slightly, a gesture that was difficult to discern, given that her eyebrows were as white as her skin. It was a clear invitation to speak. Elissa decided to risk telling another person about her Gift. Perhaps it wasn't really a risk anymore. She had told Maya about Gertrude and had not died. It was possible that after all these years, the oath she had made to Nana had somehow worn off, or at least the consequences of breaking it had. Besides, Aesha was an otherworldly sort of person herself.

"I speak to animals," said Elissa simply. "And they speak to me."

Aesha regarded Elissa with an expression that was impossible to read.

"Then you understand my Sweetheart," she said.

"Yes," said Elissa, a little taken aback. She had expected Aesha to challenge her—to ask for proof. But, like Maya, Aesha had accepted the existence of Elissa's strange Gift without hesitation.

"What does he say?" whispered Aesha. "When he sings in my ear."

Elissa looked at the Windsinger's face. Although Aesha's features were completely still, Elissa detected an air of expectancy. Perhaps Aesha already suspected what the little bird warbled to her day and night.

" 'I love you,' " said Elissa. "That is all he ever says to you."

Suddenly, before Elissa's horrified eyes, Aesha's face went through a terrible transformation, contorting and hardening until the Windsinger's normally serene features were twisted into an expression of intense pain.

"What is it?" cried Elissa.

Aesha rose hurriedly to her feet. "Nothing, nothing," she said. She reached over her shoulder and held a hand up to the little bird, who cooed at her before obediently hopping on her finger. "Take him," she said. "His house is in the bag under my bed. I must go now." Then, before Elissa could utter a word, she left the room in a flurry of pale silk.

Elissa looked at the little bird sitting contentedly upon her finger. The bird had imprinted on Aesha, and so he would never say "I love you" to anyone else. But he would feel safe and protected with Elissa, as all animals did. She put Sweet-heart in his little cage, wondering what on earth was wrong with Aesha. Then she lay down, and before she knew it, she was fast asleep.

The next morning, when Elissa awoke, she realized Aesha had not returned. Sweetheart was still perched in his little "house," as Aesha had called it, his head turned around and his beak tucked into his back feathers.

"Where has she gone?" asked Elissa.

The bird ruffled his feathers and blinked. "Away," he chirped disconsolately. "She has left me all alone."

"I'll take good care of you until she comes back," Elissa reassured the little creature.

The bird looked at Elissa, first out of one eye, then out of the other, his messy little head feathers askew. If the creature hadn't looked so mournful, it would have been comical.

"She isn't coming back," said the bird.

"What do you mean?" asked Elissa. "Of course she is."

"No," said the bird sadly. "I shall never see my love again. She has flown to the Mountain to die."

# ✎ 9 ✎

# The Great Circle

"I have to find Aesha," insisted Elissa. "It's very important."

The Captain regarded Elissa without a trace of sympathy, his lips pressed into a tight, thin line. Even when he was sitting, he seemed to be looking down his long, bony nose at her. The Captain's general air of haughtiness was increased by the fact that his eyes, which were a particularly chilly shade of blue, were always half shut. She still did not know his name.

"And I have to take you back to Castlemar," he said firmly, "which is even *more* important." Indeed it was, even if it meant that he would lose his captain's license for ordering the King's daughter to be thrown overboard. Losing his job was a fate infinitely preferable to losing his life, which was a distinct possibility should he fail to return the Princess safely to her father.

Elissa could see that pressuring the Captain was not going to be productive. So she simply wished him a good day and retreated. She walked back to the inn with a heavy step, thinking steadily about what the little bird had told her. She berated herself for not being more perceptive. Aesha had even said it herself—she wished to join her spirit to the Great Wind. There were no other Windsingers left, and Elissa had seen with her own eyes how much Aesha had faded during her stay at Castelmar. Now that Sweetheart had said she was going to the Great Circle to die, everything seemed perfectly obvious—and inevitable. Except that Elissa was not going to let it happen.

"I won't let her do it," she promised the little bird.

In spite of the fact that they had never been particularly close, Elissa felt deeply committed to Aesha. Perhaps this was because Aesha was part of Om Chai's prophecy—at least according to Maya. If the Fates had led her to Aesha, then there must be a good reason for them to stay together.

But in truth, her motivations lay elsewhere. Elissa's heart had been deeply stirred that night in Gravesport when she had first heard Aesha's haunting cry. Aesha had never made that sound again. But Elissa could still remember it, and when she did, her soul ached. *Aesha must not die,* she told herself. Elissa would make her see that there was a reason to live. After all, she had the love of her Sweetheart. He was only a little bird, but his love was pure, and very real.

"We'll find a way to go after her," she told the bird. She'd kept Sweetheart on her shoulder all morning, hoping that being close to her would comfort him, but the bird remained silent.

Elissa entered the inn, expecting to find the common room cold and empty, as usual. To her surprise, a fire was blazing away in the hearth. The small room was steaming hot and packed with people distributing winter garb—heavy boots, thick hooded jackets, woolen pants. The innkeeper, a mousy little man with a sly mouth, ran to and fro, bearing trays of ale and fresh bread for his customers.

"Northern expedition," he whispered, noticing Elissa standing by the door. "Good business."

An expedition! That sounded very promising to Elissa. "Where are they going?" she inquired as the innkeeper buzzed by with his loaded tray.

"Great Circle," he replied breathlessly. He took a moment to point his elbow toward a man who sat hunkered by the fire. "There's the leader."

What good fortune! Just when she needed some assistance, here it was! Elissa wove her way through the crowd, skirting laden packs and rolls of bedding. From the sheer quantity of baggage, it appeared the expedition was preparing for a long trip to the North.

"Sir," she said when she neared the man. "I have heard you are going to the Great Circle."

The leader sat with his broad back to her, so when he did not answer, Elissa assumed that he had not heard. She cleared her throat and prepared to speak again.

"Don't bother," snarled the leader. "I heard you the first time." He turned around to face her. "What do you want?"

Elissa was prepared for anything—a denial, a discussion, a negotiation—but not for a bear. He reared up to his full height, about seven feet, and bristled at her. Elissa was confused. She'd always gotten along fairly well with bears, but this one was conducting himself in a completely unacceptable manner.

"Don't be rude," she said sternly. "You know better than that."

At Elissa's rebuke, the bear looked very surprised, if bears can be said to produce that expression. His eyes grew so wide, they nearly popped from his head. Elissa had to laugh, which made the bear truly angry. He growled deep within his throat—and then he removed his face.

"Oh!" cried Elissa. "I mistook you for a bear."

The man stood there dumbfounded, holding a fur face mask in his hands. "Do you always talk to bears that way?" he asked with a smirk.

"No," replied Elissa, without thinking. "Usually bears are more polite. So I don't have to scold them quite so much."

The man looked down at the young woman with the copper curls and broke into great gusts of laughter. He heaved and chortled and gurgled until he gasped, and then, when he caught his breath, he laughed some more. Finally, when he was able to speak, he said, "Whatever you want from me, it's yours. I haven't had a good laugh like that in years. *Years.*"

Elissa looked up at the man she had mistaken for a bear, assessing his ability to keep a promise. "Take me to the Great Circle," she said.

It had been relatively easy to hide Elissa among the members of the expedition. She was wrapped in so many garments that nobody could possibly have guessed who she was. Boots and thick wool pants encased her lower half, while a bulky fur-lined anorak with a deep hood and a spacious front pocket obscured her upper body. Sweetheart was particularly pleased with the hood. No sooner had Elissa put on the anorak than he had crept blissfully into its warm, furry interior.

When no one was looking, Elissa carefully tucked her little pouch containing the shard beneath her undershirt, keeping it close to her heart. She'd learned a lesson from her previous mistake in Alhamazar, and even though none of these people looked like thieves, she didn't want any of them thinking she carried a money purse.

The leader, whose name turned out to be Griff, gave her a large pack, into which she placed her meager possessions: her skirt and brown cloak, which she rolled up into a tight ball; the monk's hood; her comb and undergarments; the fibula Sohar had given her at the Great Oasis; and finally, her gloves and face mask, along with kindling and some food. Everyone carried kindling and food, even the leader.

After she'd finished packing, Elissa regarded the small canvas bag she'd brought with her. It was now empty, except for the map of the world she had taken from the library. Surely the map would be ruined if she simply shoved it into her pack, where it would jostle against all the other supplies. She decided to wrap the sturdy canvas bag around the rolled-up map, tucking the cloth securely around the two ends. Then she carefully placed the bundle among her clothing so it wouldn't get crushed.

*That should do it*, she thought. *Every explorer needs a map, especially on her first trip into the unknown.*

As Griff frequently pointed out, this trip into the unknown was going to be particularly difficult and dangerous. They were going to scale the highest peak of the Great Circle.

"You are mad," he had told Elissa after she had repeated her desire to go to the Great Circle.

"I've heard that before," she replied. "Recently, in fact."

Griff snorted, unimpressed. "Well, you'll never make it. But I'll take your money."

The leader had been true to his word. Elissa's request was granted, but it came with a price. A gold piece. Fortunately, Elissa had one coin left in the hem of her brown cloak. Gold was a lot to ask, as Griff well knew, but expeditions of this type were exorbitantly expensive. Everything had to be hauled up the mountain—food, kindling, shelter—and the six porters who were to accompany them to the top demanded ample compensation. The payment, made in advance, was intended to support the porters' families in case they died en route—which, regrettably, was all too likely. The winds that howled around the Great Circle were strong enough to blow a man clear off the face of the earth.

Elissa thought that Griff would question her at length about her reasons for wanting to embark on such a dangerous journey, which would have been awkward. Confronted with questions, she would have been forced to reveal her true identity as Princess of Castlemar. Contrary to Elissa's expectations, however, Griff did not ask Elissa a thing about her mission. In fact, it didn't seem to matter to him at all where Elissa was going, or why, which suited Elissa quite well. She was curious as to why Griff was willing to risk his own life on the journey, but she hesitated to ask. Perhaps the reason he did not question her was that he himself was on some secret, or illicit, mission. Eventually, though, her curiosity got the better of her and she felt compelled to ask him why he was climbing the highest mountain on earth. To her surprise, Griff did not hesitate to reply.

"Because it is there," he said.

Elissa thought that was a ridiculous answer, but she nodded her head politely. In her mind, being "there" wasn't enough of a reason for doing anything at all, let alone risking one's life and the lives of others.

The first phase of the journey was easy, for the incline was not too steep and the path was packed hard from the long winter. Elissa felt confident that they would catch up with Aesha soon.

After all, they were only a day behind. There was no question in Elissa's mind that Aesha was heading for the highest reaches of the Great Circle. Where else would a Windsinger call home? Elissa was sure that once they had caught up with her, she could easily dissuade Aesha from her ill-conceived mission. With an optimism born of total ignorance, Elissa predicted that before the week was up, she would be back in Northport, safe and sound with Aesha in tow. At least that was what she whispered to Sweetheart, who moped a bit less, now that he was on his way to regaining his lost love.

"I can't believe you're bringing a bird with you," said Griff. He was the only member of the group who had spoken with her. Elissa later discovered that the porters, mountain people of the Far North, did not speak Common Tongue.

"He's not any bother," replied Elissa defensively. "And birds bring good luck."

Griff snorted into his beard. "Luck!" he scoffed. He pointed toward the great crown of peaks that lay before them, gleaming brilliantly in the light of midday. "To conquer mountains like those, you don't need *luck*. You need strength, stamina, and intelligence." He stared down at Elissa as if to say, *And you possess none of these qualities.*

Elissa wondered what Griff meant by "conquer." *A mountain cannot be defeated,* she thought; *it is not an enemy.* And simply climbing one did not give a person proprietary rights. People, on the other hand, could be conquered, owned, bent to one's will. Did he think of the mountain as a person? Griff's attitude perplexed her. She tried not to think about it too much, though, and focused instead on how she would bring Aesha back.

What bothered her was the fact that Aesha had run off with no warm clothes whatsoever. She had been wearing nothing but her silk dress, and even in the foothills of the Great Circle, the air was chilly and sharp with the scent of snow. How was she going to survive with so little protection against the elements? She imagined that Windsingers would dress much as the porters did—in heavy jackets, leggings, hats—as they lived in much the same climate. Elissa worried that when she finally found

Aesha, the Windsinger would be ill and in need of special care. From the way Griff talked and from the fixed, maniacal gleam in his eye that appeared whenever he gazed ahead at the mountains, she doubted he would consent to halting his expedition in order to take an ailing woman back to Northport. She fretted throughout that day and the next. Then, the following day, she fretted because she could not find a single trace of Aesha's passage, no matter how hard she looked.

*Where's Favian when you need him?* she thought.

On the fourth day they began their ascent up the rocky, windblown slopes. There was still no sign of anyone's having passed that way recently.

"Are you sure this is the way?" Elissa asked Griff.

"Well," he said slowly, rubbing his beard thoughtfully. "There is one other way."

Elissa's heart sank. There was another trail! She had thought that there was only one route to the Great Circle. What if Aesha had taken another? As Elissa tramped alongside Griff, attempting to match his pace, she despaired. At this very moment Aesha might be perishing on some lonesome rocky trail, cold and worn-out with hunger.

"You can fly," he said with a snort of laughter. Then he clapped Elissa on the back so hard that he knocked Sweetheart clean off her shoulder. The bird fluttered around Elissa's head, irritated at having been dislodged. "It's great having you along for this trip," he said. "You're always good for a laugh. You and Feather Face, there."

"I'm so glad I can be of service," muttered Elissa. But the sarcasm was lost on Griff, who had already forged ahead. Somehow, he always wound up first in line.

On the fifth day, the trail became considerably steeper and the air blew in sudden sharp gusts off the sides of the great mountains. For the first time, she felt the sting of snow against her cheeks.

"Raise your hood and put on your face mask," ordered Griff. "Otherwise you'll lose your skin."

Elissa did as she was told, tucking Sweetheart under her hair for his protection. "Stay there," she whispered to him. "It's too cold for you out here." The little bird fluffed his feathers and retreated, more than happy to be out of the wind.

That evening, after a grueling day of crawling up fields of loose scree, they came to a stone hut. "The lodge," announced Griff.

The "lodge" looked more like a pile of rubble than a building, but it offered some protection from the winds that had now begun to howl down the sides of the mountain. The shelter was so small that at first Elissa thought they wouldn't all fit inside. But, with considerable crowding and shoving, they all managed to squeeze into the hut. The porters soon got a fire going on the dirt floor. After the evening meal had been consumed, the porters simply fell asleep where they sat. Elissa looked around in vain for a place to stretch out.

"Don't even think of going outside," warned Griff. "You'll be dead by morning."

*Dead?* If spending one night outside would kill Elissa, who had plenty of meat on her bones, what would happen to Aesha, who didn't even seem to have *skin* on her bones?

The next morning, Elissa awoke cramped and sore from her night on the bare earth. She was stiff and aching from days of climbing, and her thighs felt as if they had been replaced by blocks of wood. She raised herself up very slowly into a sitting position. The porters were already gathering up their packs and drinking some absolutely foul-smelling tea. They sat huddled together, like so many black-braided, broad-chested peas in a pod. Elissa wrinkled up her nose when one of the porters offered her a cup. The man said something.

"He says it's warming," said Griff. "Go ahead, it won't kill you."

Elissa took the cup hesitantly. The porter, with his steeply angled burnished cheeks, looked at her impassively from under his heavy eyelids. She sipped. The tea tasted as foul as it smelled, but, as promised, a moment later a slow warmth spread throughout her body. She felt good. The porter smiled in an unexpectedly friendly manner. He clasped her very briefly on the arm before moving on.

"They are concerned for you," said Griff. Elissa wanted to ask why, but she had tea in her mouth. "This morning we begin our final ascent," continued Griff. Elissa must have looked startled, or as startled as a person can look with a mouth full of dirty socks. "Haven't you looked outside?" he asked.

They had arrived so late last night, and she had been so tired, that she had not even noticed how close they were to the peaks of the Great Circle. Elissa poked her head through the rough door frame and sucked in her breath. Before her lay a shimmering expanse of white, rising upward in a smooth, unbroken slope. To see the tip of the peak, she had to tilt her head straight back. Even then she could only spot part of it, for the winds continually kicked up a cloud of white crystals that obscured the summit.

"Wuayra Takiy," said Griff. " 'Where the Wind Sings.' " His voice, usually rough, was almost soft with reverence. "The tallest mountain in the world."

Elissa smiled. It was a fitting name. "Why are the porters concerned about me?" she asked, remembering that Griff had not explained.

"They think you are going to die today," said Griff. "And so do I. Let's go."

Six hours later, Elissa thought she was going to die as well. The expedition had come to the second "lodge," a tumbled heap of stones even smaller than the first. Elissa crawled through the doorway on all fours, which was a position she was beginning to hate, having spent the last few hours crawling up the steep slopes of Where the Wind Sings on her hands and knees. When she sat on the floor, the world spun blackly around her. Someone handed her a mug.

"Altitude sickness," said Griff. There were mumblings from the porters. Elissa sipped at the foul concoction, which helped ease the dizziness.

"This is as far as you go," said Griff.

"No," said Elissa, straining to see through the darkness that filled her eyes. "I have to go with you."

"What do you want from me, girl?" cried Griff, exasperated. "I've taken you farther than anybody else could have. Look! Look out there! What do you see?"

Elissa struggled to regain her footing. She peered out from the doorway, into an amorphous shifting cloud that completely obscured her vision. It looked as though a solid wall of mist had been erected in front of their door, cutting them completely off from the rest of world. For all she knew, there was nothing beyond it. Elissa felt nauseous.

"You can't go on," said Griff. "You're already too sick, and you'll only slow me down. Just wait here for us. We'll leave enough provisions to last for two days. By then we'll be back."

Elissa was too weak to reply, so she simply sat down again. The porters, after eating some food, packed up. One of them, probably the same man who had given her the tea earlier, handed her a little woven bag filled with smelly leaves and said something to her. His dark eyes were kind.

"He says you are to drink the tea twice a day," said Griff. "And he says you will find what you are looking for."

Griff gave Elissa an odd look as he translated. It was finally occurring to him, through the fog of his own self-involvement, that Elissa may have had a good reason for wanting to climb Where the Wind Sings. He shook his head. Whatever her reason may have been, he didn't want to know it. His own purpose, kept safely hidden from the prying eyes of strangers, was enough for him. He was known in the North as an adventurer, but the reason he was climbing the mountain was not, as he had claimed, to scale its height just because it was "there." Griff was driven by the desire to find something he had lost among the misty peaks of the Great Circle a long, long time ago. Sometimes he wondered if what he sought still existed. But until he knew for certain, until he had seen for himself that every peak was bare, he would not give up. Griff bade Elissa farewell, told her to stay inside, and said he would be back tomorrow, after he had "conquered" the greatest mountain of them all.

To be truthful, it didn't really matter to Elissa whether Griff stayed or left. She was too sick to care. She couldn't even remember why she had asked to come along on this fool's mission. Elissa slept, utterly exhausted. When she awoke, she felt a little better. She prepared some tea and assessed her situation.

"I am stuck on the world's highest mountain," she said out loud. She nodded her head slowly, checking to see if it would fall off. It did not. She rose and found her feet surprisingly strong. She took a deep breath. "I feel fine," she said to the floor. "They should have taken me." Elissa walked to the doorway and squinted at the nothingness that lay outside. Even she had to admit it was hopeless. One wrong step and she could end up falling onto Northport.

All at once, and entirely without warning, the

white cloud lifted. Elissa found herself gazing at infinity. She gasped. The whole world lay at her feet—all of it. She saw clear down the side of the mountain to Northport, the town she had left six days earlier. And beyond Northport, the coastline stretched on forever. To her utter amazement, she spotted the turrets of far-off Castlemar! And beyond its battlements was another port, which she thought at first might be Southport, where, by now, Maya's ship would be berthed. But Southport was perhaps too far away to be seen, even from this great height. To her left, the Great Sea covered the world. And to her right, the mountains marched row upon row down to the hills that eventually flattened into the gently rolling terrain of the Far North. She could even make out a patch of forest. That was probably the range that flanked High Crossing. It was exhilarating, seeing so much all at once. Now she knew what it must be like to be an eagle. She'd know what to talk about the next time she met one.

Elissa turned and looked beyond the hut, toward the peak of Where the Wind Sings, its snowy summit a brilliant, eye-searing white against the bluest sky in the world. Seven tiny dots were stretched along the mountain's magnificent flank. From this distance they looked like ants laboring up a sugar hill. Elissa reentered the small shelter and rummaged around among the provisions Griff had left her. She placed the bag of tea, some kindling and food, and a blanket into her pack, which she hoisted over her shoulders.

"It's time to go find Aesha," she told Sweetheart as she tucked him into her hood. Then she pulled down her face mask and walked out the door, taking the path straight to the summit.

*Besides,* she thought, *I, too, would like to touch the sky.*

## ➻ 10 ➻

# Where the Wind Sings

Elissa trudged slowly up the trail to the summit. She placed her feet with great care, so as to conserve her energy and prevent a reoccurrence of altitude sickness. As she climbed, she examined the terrain for signs of Aesha. Ever since Griff had told her the name of the mountain, she had been sure this was Aesha's intended destination, though for the life of her, she couldn't imagine how Aesha was managing. Even with the heavy wool pants, the boots, the bulky coat, the hood, and the face mask, it was bitterly cold. In spite of her discomfort, every so often Elissa stopped to take in the view. It was absolutely incredible. At times she had to sit down to look, for she was so close to the top of the earth, she felt as though at any moment she might soar off the mountain and fall *up*—into the sky. It was a strange, almost unnerving, feeling. She had suddenly lost substance; it was as though she weighed nothing.

With every step Elissa took, even more of the world was revealed to her astounded eyes. Fantastically, for it seemed unbelievable, she began to make out the edges of the desert. And in the ocean she saw islands—little ones close to the shore, to the south. And could that be Gravesport? Elissa began to have some comprehension of Griff's desire to climb a mountain simply because it was there.

What struck her most as she climbed was how much of what she was seeing resembled her map. Of course, technically speaking, the map wasn't hers at all; it was her father's. She had merely stolen it. She crawled up the side of the mountain, making the final ascent with the map on her mind.

"It doesn't look like a bowl," she proclaimed as she looked out toward the horizon. "It looks more like a plate, a round plate." Yet as she climbed even higher, she began to rethink that theory as well, for the horizon was beginning to develop a distinct convex curve. *Perhaps it is shaped like a bean pot after all,* she thought. *In which case, why don't we fall off the sides? And how does the ocean stay put?* She stood up to take a good look at the world, perhaps to settle the matter in her mind once and for all. She could see the entire coast at that point: the ports, the flatlands, and far, far out to sea, a little dot, perhaps an island. For some reason, that small dot fascinated her. It was out of place, that little bump on the horizon. She was focusing all her attention on it, trying to make out whether it was actually a piece of land or merely a trick of the light glancing off the far reaches of the sea. Perhaps it was where the monster lived at the end of the world. Or maybe it was Maya's island. These puzzles preoccupied her and provided distraction from thoughts of the long climb ahead. At this point she was almost used to crawling on all fours.

"This isn't so bad," she said.

The storm hit less than five minutes later.

At first she didn't realize what was happening. She had been thinking about the map, and about plates, bowls, and bean pots, when, in a flash, everything—the glinting sea, the land, the islands, the sky, and even the mountain— completely disappeared.

At first Elissa tried to stay upright. She was so shocked by the suddenness of the storm—the noise, the immense power of the wind—that she could not think. When a gust lifted her right off her feet, she realized she should make herself as flat as possible. She dropped to the ground, spread-eagled. Even in that position, it was difficult to stay down. Elissa found herself trying to sink her fingers into the snow, struggling to find protection against the icy fists smashing at her from every direction. She cried out in fear, but the wind swept her voice away even before the sound emerged from her mouth. There was nothing to do but shut her eyes against the blinding white gale and hold on for dear life.

*What now?* she thought.

"Go back," said a familiar, faint voice.

It was amazing to Elissa that she could hear anything at all with the shrieking of the wind, but the tiny voice came through as clearly as if it were speaking directly into her ear. It probably was.

*You again,* she thought. She wanted to ask where the moth had been for so long, but now was not the time. If she didn't obey quickly, she would surely perish out here in the snows. Besides, she could not speak.

Elissa backed down the slope as best she could, inch by inch. There were times she felt the mountain heave under her, like a balky horse trying to shake off an unwelcome rider, but she held on and continued to push herself slowly backward, like a crab. Her hands were numb by now, and her arms and legs ached with the strain. She was blind and deaf. *This is impossible,* she thought. *I'll never make it.* Then she hit a patch of sheer ice and began to slide uncontrollably down the steep slope.

"Aaaahhhh!" she cried as she desperately scrabbled for a hold. But it was no use; she slid faster and faster.

*This is it,* she thought. *I am falling, falling off the top of the world. Falling into the sky.* She could feel Sweetheart's fragile body shuddering against the back of her neck. *Soon it will be over,* she thought, *and I will see the world as birds do. Only I don't have wings.*

Then, all at once, Elissa's stomach grazed against pebbles, which slowed her somewhat. Soon afterward, her feet hit something solid.

For a moment or two she lay stunned. Her break-neck slide had stopped, but she still felt the mountain whizzing by. She began to explore the ground with her feet. Boulders! It must be another shelter. Elissa doubled herself up until she could touch the wall with her fingers. Something wasn't right. She felt the resistance of the wall, but not the surface. *I've lost my fingers,* she thought. But they were all there. Only the feeling had gone.

She made her way along the wall inch by inch until she came to a hard, planed surface—a wooden door. Elissa wedged her shoulder against it and pushed with all her strength. Then she tried pulling it with her numb hands, but the door did not yield.

*It must be latched,* thought Elissa. She fumbled along the sides of the door, but her fingers were useless. Even if the door had a latch, she would not be able to lift it. She slid her hands down the side of the door until she felt something dangling stiffly—a latchstring. Elissa wrapped her hands around the string, but the wind snatched it from her useless frozen fingers time and time again. Finally, she bent over and took the string between her teeth. With a jerk of her head, the latch released. Elissa leaned against the door and pushed into it, aided by the wind as much as by her own weight. At last it swung open. Elissa tumbled inside, where she lay panting on the hard earth floor.

*We're safe.* She tried to reassure Sweetheart, but no sound came out of her mouth. *First the wind stole my fingers,* she thought. *Now it's got my voice.*

The wind had stolen enough voice to fill the whole world. It shrieked and screamed and howled around the shelter. And it followed Elissa, pushing through the open door, slamming it against the rock wall until the door cracked into pieces. Then the wind flew about the room in a furious rush, seeking her. Elissa covered her head with her arms and attempted to crawl on her elbows and knees, but even inside the hut the wind knocked her down. She rolled from one end of the room to the other, until she was finally out of the direct line of the doorway, away from the grasp of the wind. Still it found her, replacing her warmth with its coldness, her voice with its howl, her sight with its blinding whiteness, her sensation with nothing—nothing at all.

*This is it,* thought Elissa. *I'm going to die.* She felt a brief pang of regret for leaving her green valley and its high, flower-filled meadows. The realization that she would never see another flower again filled her heart with intense sorrow. *Oh,* she thought, *if only . . .*

Elissa felt a faint movement jostle her out-stretched hand. A delicate tendril pushed its way through the compact earth of the shelter floor. It was tipped with a little bud. Slowly the bud un-furled to reveal a feathery, daisy-like blossom.

"Oh dear," Elissa whispered. She had forgotten to control her thoughts, her feelings. She tried to curl her body around the delicate bloom in a vain attempt to protect it. "You aren't sup-posed to be here."

*And neither are you,* said Nana.

*Nana?* Elissa tried to sit up, but she couldn't move, couldn't see in the gloom.

*I sent you on an errand and here you are, stuck on some out-of-the-way mountain. You are* late, *child.*

*Late for what?*

*The end of the world,* said Nana matter-of-factly.

*Oh, right. I forgot that the world was ending.*

186

Om Chai's prophecy suddenly seemed painfully imminent.

*Just make sure you remember to fetch me what I asked for.*

Elissa laughed, a hoarse little rasp. *You'll have to send someone else this time . . . I'm ending, too.*

*So be it,* howled the wind.

Elissa felt a small movement at the back of her neck. The little bird crept slowly through her tangled hair and poked its messy head out from under Elissa's hood. *Oh, poor dear thing,* she tried to say. *I should never have brought you here.* But her voice came out in an unintelligible croak. Then, to her horror, she felt a slight pressure on her neck as the bird prepared for flight.

"No!" she whispered. But it was too late. With a flutter of gray wings, the small bird launched itself and flew straight toward the swirling white wall beyond the doorway. Elissa felt the faint brush of his wings against her cheek before his last plaintive cry—"My love!"—was swallowed by the maelstrom.

Elissa squeezed her eyes shut. She could not feel anything anymore, except for the breaking of her heart.

"Sweetheart," she whispered. "Come back."

"I'm right here," said a voice. She felt herself being lifted by a pair of arms, and then there was warmth, and pain—terrible, burning pain.

A tall, pale figure stood at the pinnacle of Wuayra Takiy, a peak so unimaginably high that its summit had earned a name of its own, Hanan Pacha: Sky. *All human names are poor substitutes for the real thing,* she thought, for this was a place where human feet had never trod, and which had never been claimed by any king. Nor would it be, for Sky has no boundaries and no limits.

"Take me," said the Windsinger.

She waited for the Winds to come, but they did not, for the Song no longer burst forth from her throat to call the Great Wind to her.

"Take me!" she called. "I must join you." This time there was an answering gust.

The Windsinger prepared herself. Soon it would be time to give her Spirit to the Great Wind. She was happy, for now her ancestors would receive her, and at last her loneliness would end. She opened her arms, ready for the

Great Wind to carry her up into the sky, ready to meld into its howling fury. She felt the Wind stir, but it was not for her.

Looking down, she saw a line of men toiling up the side of the mountain they called Where the Wind Sings. Around them, the Wind had started to roil and turn.

"No!" she cried. "Not them! I am the one!"

The Wind began to churn and grind even as she screamed her protest. As she watched, it built into the tempest that is called the Great Wind. The Great Song.

"Come to me!" she cried again. But the Wind would not hear her plea. It had chosen another.

As the Wind increased its force, the lone figure at the summit remained erect, for no wind could ever knock her down. No wind could make her bend. She stood, head high, amid the rising plumes of white snow, a length of pale silk whipping and snapping about her. Perhaps her throat could no longer produce the Song, but she still heard its melody, felt its rhythm. She closed her eyes and listened. The Song had changed. A new melody, singing in high counterpoint to the Wind, came to her ears. She heard the voices of her ancestors, the chorus that was no more but which still sang on the summit of Sky.

"Stay," they sang. "It is not your time. Open your mouth and take our Song!"

"Who will join you, then?" she cried. "For whom do you sing?"

The Wind shrieked and howled all around her, but with a controlled force that only suggested its true power.

*"For the thief,"* sang the chorus. *"The one who stole our young."*

Then the gale struck, releasing its full strength, and the straggling line of men was obliterated by the force of the Song.

As she opened her mouth to breathe in the Song, she saw something flit past her. It was Griff, rising into the sky to join the chorus of the Windsingers he had destroyed so long ago. Taking him was not revenge, for the Windsingers would never sing in anger, not even to this man. Rather, gathering him up to them was the fulfillment of Griff's ultimate desire. For, like so many men, the drive to possess the unattainable had led him to destroy those he cherished most, and in so doing he had lost his own Spirit.

The tall figure watched as the chorus chose its sacrifice, spinning him high into the air until he touched the sky, laughing.

Elissa screamed as sensation returned to her limbs.

"Slowly," said a soft voice. "Don't warm her all at once."

The pain retreated. Then it came again, and again, but each time it waned in intensity. Finally, she felt only warmth.

"I don't think she will lose any fingers or toes," said the voice. "But she will need to stay warm from now on."

"That won't be a problem," said another voice, deeper than the first.

Elissa wanted to open her eyes, but found she couldn't. Something was pressed against her face, arms, and legs, binding her so tightly that she could not move.

"She still feels so cold," said the deep voice.

Elissa struggled to free herself, and her bonds were released. When she leaned back, she found herself looking directly into a pair of worried, dark eyes.

*It's you,* she tried to say. But her voice came out as a croak.

"Hush," said Favian. "Can you drink some tea?"

Elissa nodded. Favian reluctantly eased his grip on her, just enough to lift a cup of tea to Elissa's mouth.

"Sip it slowly," he said.

Elissa did as she was told, taking in the hot liquid one sip at a time. The pungent aroma was as revolting as always, but never had drinking a brew that smelled like dirty socks held more appeal. Slowly, her frozen interior thawed and she felt a resurgence of life.

"That's better," he said.

"How did you find me?" asked Elissa. Her voice was back. It felt wonderful. "And don't you dare say 'Long experience as a hunter.'"

Favian grinned sheepishly. He had been about to utter those very words. "Well," he said. "When your father sent word to Leonne that you had disappeared, I came as quickly as I could. He had already dispatched a ship to the South, so I decided to search for you in the North. Once I arrived in Northport, it was easy. I simply followed the trail that the innkeeper said the expedition had taken."

"But how did you survive the storm?"

Favian looked at Elissa—at her dry, peeling lips, her feverish eyes, her skin mottled and raw from the wind and cold, and he wanted to gather her up in his arms again. "I am not much affected by cold," he said at last. "Nor, it seems, is Aesha."

Aesha was sitting next to Favian, looking very much as she had the last time Elissa had seen her, except now she was smiling. Seeing Aesha brought back the last image Elissa could remember— little gray wings snatched up by the wind.

"Oh, Aesha!" cried Elissa. "Sweetheart is gone. I lost him in the storm."

Favian's heart stopped in mid-beat. He hadn't thought that Elissa might have been accompanied . . . by a suitor.

"Don't fret," said Aesha comfortingly. "Sweetheart came to me." Elissa heard a warbling "I love you" as the little bird poked its head through Aesha's downy hair. Aesha smiled.

Favian looked confused. "Sweetheart?"

"Yes," said Aesha. "Sweetheart is my little bird."

For some reason, Favian was frowning. Elissa

imagined he was probably thinking how silly it was of her to bring a tropical bird to the top of the world's highest mountain.

"I know it was stupid to bring him," said Elissa. "But I couldn't leave him behind, and Aesha was going to . . ."

Elissa stopped speaking. For her friend's sake, she shouldn't reveal what Sweetheart had said. And how could she explain, anyway? She couldn't very well tell Favian that a little bird had told her.

"I came back to die," said Aesha.

Favian looked at her curiously.

The Windsinger paused, searching for the words. She looked at Elissa and saw a spark of understanding in the girl's eyes.

"You aren't fading anymore," said Elissa. It was true. Although Aesha was as pale as ever, she was solid. She had lost her transparency. "What happened? Did you find your people?"

Aesha smiled enigmatically. "In a way," she said. The Windsinger's vision turned inward; in her eyes there was a swirl of snow, then scuttling gray clouds, the kind that run before a storm. Then they turned a deep, vivid blue—the color of the sky on a summer afternoon.

"I realized there was something I needed to do," she said at last.

"What?" asked Elissa.

"I don't know yet," replied Aesha. "But when I discover what it is, I will be with you. Of that I am certain."

Favian also shared Aesha's presentiment, though he didn't quite understand it. For now, he was just happy that Elissa's "sweetheart" was only a little bird.

Favian took Elissa by the hand. "As will I," he said. "No matter what befalls us."

## ❧ 11 ❧

# Pirates

The journey down the mountain was, in some respects, more difficult than the ascent had been, for Elissa could barely walk. At the hut, Favian had constructed a sling out of a large piece of canvas and a length of rope that had been abandoned there by an earlier expedition. Once the canvas was securely lashed around Elissa, he was able to drag her over the icy stretches. It was cumbersome, somewhat like dragging a large cocoon, but the sling worked well until the ice began to give way to rough ground.

"I'll have to carry you the rest of the way," Favian said. He was standing on the edge of the ice field, his feet melting the dirty crystals into steaming puddles. "It isn't much farther to Northport."

Elissa looked up at Favian. He had his profile

turned to her, but she could see the weariness in his eyes as he surveyed the journey yet to come.

"It's miles," she said. "I can walk. Unlash me."

Favian gave her a look so filled with concern that Elissa's heart was touched. Something about Favian had changed. She didn't know what had happened to him in Leonne, but he seemed less arrogant. Perhaps regaining his title had given him a measure of security. As Elissa well knew, Favian's whole world depended on titles.

"I will walk," she said again, firmly. "I can do it." Elissa slid her hand into her pocket, where the courageous little flower still blossomed. She had made Favian dig it out of the earth for her with the tip of his sword. And he had done so without the faintest protest.

Favian helped Elissa out of the sling and onto her feet. She stood up shakily and took a few wobbling steps.

"Let me carry you," he said, reaching out for her.

Elissa cast him a determined look. "Give me a chance," she said. After a few more steps, she felt some strength return to her legs. "You see?" she said. "I'm fine."

Reluctantly, Favian let Elissa walk, though he stayed very close to her, ready to grasp her arm whenever she stumbled. Aesha walked ahead of them. Elissa noticed that wherever Aesha put her feet, even in the snow, they left no mark.

"I bet you couldn't track *her*," whispered Elissa.

Favian looked at Aesha, and at the trail she didn't leave. "No," he replied honestly. "I couldn't. No one can track the wind." He looked at Elissa. "But I can always track you," he said. "And that's the only thing that really matters."

Elissa did not ask why it mattered, for they were coming down to the path leading to North-port, and she had noticed something in the harbor—a ship flying the royal flag of Castlemar.

Elissa had no idea what she was going to say to her father. On the one hand, she was ashamed of herself for having run away. It was, in retrospect, a childish and cowardly thing to do. Her disappearance had, no doubt, caused a great deal of fuss in Castlemar. But on the other hand, Elissa had no intention of letting Falk rule her life with the same uncompromising attitude with which he ruled the rest of his subjects. After all, he had planned to announce her engagement to a total stranger, and in front of his entire court, without so much as a by-your-leave. Elissa suddenly remembered that she was fifteen now. Her birthday had completely slipped her mind. She drew herself up as tall as she could as they approached Northport's inn, which, after her ascent of Where the Wind Sings, looked like a palace.

It was strange, but Northport seemed to have changed in her absence. The houses looked so much better kept than when she had left. There were carriages, carts, horses, clothes drying in courtyards, fences—all the trappings of human occupancy. Everything looked so . . . civilized.

When they came to the inn, Favian stopped her. "I don't know what this is all about," he said, casting a meaningful glance at the royal guards flanking the door. "I mean, between you and your father. But if you'd like me to stay, I will."

Elissa considered his offer. Her dispute with her father was personal, but Favian had just saved her life. And, by rights, he should know why it was she had left Castlemar. She thought of telling him right then and there, but realized that she would not have enough time to explain everything. It was likely her father had already been informed of her arrival, and was at this very moment waiting for Elissa to appear.

"Yes," she said. "Stay with me, Favian. And you too, Aesha."

Aesha smiled slightly and nodded. "I have no intention of leaving you again," she said. They entered the room together. There was a man sitting by the fire—and a young girl.

"Elissa!" A jubilant cry broke forth from Maya's lips as she catapulted herself toward Elissa.

"Maya!" cried Elissa, hugging her tightly. "What are you doing here?"

"Gertrude's here, too. I brought her," babbled the little girl, not answering Elissa's question. "But not Ralph. Gertrude wouldn't let him on the boat." Maya whispered hoarsely into Elissa's ear. "She *said* something to him."

"What?" Elissa was making a monumental effort to grasp what Maya was saying. Her mind still felt numb.

"How should *I* know?"

King Falk rose from his chair.

Elissa gently freed herself from Maya's grasp. "My lord." Elissa greeted him formally. She offered him neither the deference of a curtsy nor the warmth of a smile.

"Elissa," said Falk. He looked as though he wanted to embrace her, but didn't dare. "I am so glad you are safe."

There was an awkward pause, which Gertrude filled by muscling her way into the inn and braying at the top of her lungs. Elissa threw her arms around Gertrude's neck, breathing into the donkey's shaggy mane with delight.

She didn't even notice the innkeeper, who Gertrude had unceremoniously dragged behind her.

"Blasted donkey," Favian muttered though clenched teeth. "What has *she* got that I haven't got?"

"Your Majesty!" cried the innkeeper, panting. "I could not stop the beast." The little man was still holding on to Gertrude's tether, valiantly pulling at it while simultaneously pushing Gertrude's rump, neither of which the donkey was responding to.

Falk regarded the group—donkey; little girl;

tall, pale creature; disheveled young man; and the Princess of Castlemar. His daughter, who was standing as firmly before him as the mountain she had just scaled, who looked as unmovable as her donkey, and who deserved his apology.

Elissa watched her father, waiting for him to say something. For the first time, Elissa noticed that there were wrinkles around his eyes, a few gray hairs at his temples. He seemed to have aged since she saw him last. He looked at her, but did not speak. Apparently, he was leaving it to Elissa to break the silence, to make the first move.

As always, Elissa had a great deal of difficulty devising strategies in games of personal power. It was simply not in her nature. When she finally spoke, she could do nothing other than state the truth.

"These are my friends," Elissa said simply. "They will stay with me for as long as they like."

Falk nodded.

"And as for a husband, I will wed *who* I please, *when* I please," Elissa continued, her voice growing stronger. On this particular matter, she would not be moved, ever.

Falk nodded again. To his credit, he had

learned from his recent mistakes and would, in the future, tread gently down the path to Elissa's heart, should he ever be given the opportunity to travel it again.

While Falk sat and nodded his assent, Favian blinked vigorously. He tugged lightly on Maya's braid and bent his head. "Has there been a betrothal?" he hissed urgently. "To *whom*?"

"Shhh!" said the girl.

A silence descended upon the room. Having stated her case as clearly as she could, Elissa didn't know what else to say. Falk had nodded twice, so she supposed he had acquiesced. Was that all there was to it? Was she supposed to go back to Castlemar and try being a princess again? Suddenly all the strength left Elissa's legs. The room began to spin.

Falk jumped to his feet. He grabbed her by the elbows and quickly sat her down in the chair he had recently occupied. "I am sorry," he murmured. "I should have sat you down much sooner." He crooked a finger at the innkeeper and asked him to bring refreshments for them all.

"All?" asked the man, eyeing the donkey. Gertrude eyed him right back.

"Yes, *all*," said the King. "Now everybody please sit."

While the innkeeper scurried off to fetch warm cider, bread—and *oats,* Favian and Aesha positioned themselves on either side of Elissa. Maya plunked herself down at Elissa's feet, and Gertrude sat in the doorway. To Falk, it was as if they were protecting her—*from him.* He would be fooling himself if he believed his loyalty to Elissa matched theirs. So far, he had not proven himself to be the most trustworthy of fathers. But Elissa had spoken, and now Falk's moment of truth was upon him.

He began to speak, slowly, as though each word weighed heavily on his tongue. "I admit to you now, openly and before everyone present, that I have made a huge blunder, though I never intended to cause you any harm. My decisions concerning you have, in all respects, been based on my role as King of Castlemar, not as your father."

Elissa drew in her breath sharply and leaned forward. But Falk held up his hand in an authoritative gesture. "No, don't speak yet. I have held certain beliefs concerning how I should behave with you, notions that I now see have been misguided. You have every reason to be angry with me." Falk paused. "You have the right to choose your companions, the right to choose your husband, and the right to live your own life, wherever you may please—in Castlemar with me, or anywhere else you might choose. I give you my word." He hesitated, then added wryly, "If for no other reason than to make sure you will not attempt to scale the highest mountain in the world again."

Falk stopped and waited for Elissa's reply. It was like waiting to see whether the falcon he had just trained would return on its first flight. Sometimes fledglings simply returned to the wild, never to be seen again.

Elissa dropped her gaze, her attention now focused inward. In effect, Falk had granted her complete autonomy, and without argument. He had given her precisely what she had demanded. She could befriend whoever she chose, marry at will; she could even go home to High Crossing. She should feel happy. So why did she feel so deflated? Perhaps it was because she had not really intended to ask for his permission. She didn't need to be granted the right to live her own life. All she had wanted was for him to see her as an equal—someone who merited respect.

Falk noted her hesitation. Perhaps the fledgling was not quite ready to leave the nest. "My ship is in the harbor," he said gently. "With your consent, we will all go back to Castlemar, where you will be able to recuperate. Then you can tell me what course you have decided upon."

Elissa nodded. Suddenly, she felt so tired. She hadn't realized that she would have to make such a final decision. She looked at Falk. He didn't look imperious or angry—just sad. Maybe later, when she had rested, they would talk again. Quietly.

"If everyone else is in agreement . . . ," she said, looking around at her companions. They all nodded simultaneously—even Gertrude. Elissa thought it curious that they were looking at her as if she were their leader. One would have thought that position would be occupied by Favian. "All right," she said. "We'll go back with you." As she spoke, she felt a tiny stirring in her pocket—the gentle yearning of leaves for sunlight. "But first I have to plant a flower."

Falk's ship left Northport the following evening with no fanfare, even though everybody in town knew the King had been visiting. The monarch had requested that there be no ceremony. In any event, the townspeople were thoroughly distracted by the arrival of six porters, who excitedly told an incoherent tale of how the leader of their expedition had been carried off by a huge white bird to join the God of the Sky, Hanan Pacha. So between the distraction of the porters and the desire to conform to the King's wishes, there hadn't been a ceremony to mark their departure. Sky god or not, the King's wish was everybody's command.

That night, as he lay in his cabin, Falk wondered how to proceed, for though he had granted Elissa her freedom, including the right to renounce her claim to the throne and to return to High Crossing, he could not bear to lose her, as he had lost her mother. There was something he needed to tell her, when the moment was right—something that might convince her to stay with him.

Favian's mind was also troubled that evening. After his initial shock at discovering that Elissa had nearly been betrothed during his absence, he had begun to wonder where he stood with her. In spite of everything they had been through together, he felt that he had very little access to what was going on in her mind. He had discovered the secret of her birth, had he not? What more could there be? She had refused her father's arranged marriage, which gave Favian immense satisfaction, but was there someone else in her life? Elissa had demanded the right to choose her own mate, and her father had granted it. She could choose anybody. What if it wasn't him?

Favian felt restless and confined in his narrow bunk. He sat up and pulled on his boots. Perhaps some fresh air would help. He needed to pace.

Once on deck, he discovered that pacing was out of the question. The ship rocked and swayed in the breeze, and moreover, the object of his confusion was already on deck.

Elissa had come on deck to breathe the night air and to clear her mind as well. She had a lot to think about. Now that she had won her autonomy, she felt the need to plan her life. For quite some time now—ever since she had left High Crossing, in fact—Elissa had had the feeling that this wild train of events that had taken over her life was not under her control at all. She felt like a marionette, being twitched this way and that by unseen hands. Whose hands were they? Surely not her father's, in spite of all his attempts to direct her movements. The gods'? Considering everything that had happened to her in the past year, she was beginning to see why some people believed in them. How else could she explain the Khan, the shard, Om Chai, Maya, Aesha? And then there was Nana's "appearance" on the mountain. For a hallucination, she had sounded surprisingly real. Nana was always sending her to fetch one thing or another. But her message harkened back to Om Chai's incomprehensible prophecy, which nagged at her. There was clearly an important task she still needed to perform. Something having to do with Maya, and Aesha, and Favian.

Favian's sudden appearance on deck interrupted her thoughts. Immediately she felt guilty. Poor Favian; she hadn't explained a thing to him. It was time he knew—about everything.

"Hello, Favian," she said.

Favian looked at Elissa. Her eyes glowed in

the darkness, like two beacons marking a danger-ous shoreline. Favian had managed to bungle so many conversations with Elissa, he didn't want to repeat his past mistakes. Yet no matter what he said, things always seemed to go wrong. He took a breath.

"Good evening," he said, and immediately re-gretted his stiff opening. It would have been more natural to have said "Hello," as she had. Elissa remained silent.

"Uh," he said.

"What is it?" asked Elissa distractedly. His presence had suddenly reminded her that she had another, more immediate problem—being Prin-cess, with all its accompanying duties and re-sponsibilities, including the unwanted burden of marriage.

"I was thinking," he said. "As you know, I am officially the Count of Leonne—again. Well, about this choosing-a-husband business. Uh, did you have anybody in mind?" Favian winced. It had come out much too bluntly.

Elissa was staring at him in disbelief. Once again, she was being pressured into decisions for everyone else's benefit. She could barely contain her disappointment; there was so much she had wanted to tell him.

She turned and walked away from him without a backward glance.

Favian struck himself on the forehead until the sparks flew about his head like a swarm of bright gnats.

Elissa could not fall asleep. As she lay in her bunk, she listened to Maya's soft breathing, hoping that the steady rise and fall of the girl's breath would lull her into slumber. Maya always slept peacefully, a smile upon her lips. Elissa would give anything to sleep with such serenity tonight.

Elissa did not normally sit in judgment of herself, but she felt that she had been overly harsh with Favian. It was true that she had originally thought him arrogant and pretentious, and, as was obvious from their recent conversation, he still placed entirely too much value on social status. But when she thought back, she realized that Favian had also been unswervingly loyal, a trait that she had not adequately appreciated. He had generously, even nobly, placed himself at her service right from the very start. He had assisted her without question the night they had freed Aesha. And now that she thought about it, he had never questioned her or pried into her affairs. His gentility had probably prevented him from asking her personal questions, and she, of course, had offered him nothing. Not one word of explanation. Most embarrassing of all was the fact that he had risked his life to save hers and this evening she had cut him off, quite unfairly. She felt an apology was in order, but it was very late. Favian was probably sound asleep.

Elissa rose and threw her brown cloak over her nightdress. Gertrude had been despondent ever since they departed. Perhaps she should check on her. She was probably seasick. Or maybe she simply regretted telling Ralph to stay behind. Perhaps some familiar company would cheer them both up. A nice chat with Gertrude always helped put things into perspective.

She secured the opening of her cloak against the late-night chill with Sohar's fibula and slipped out the door, feeling her way along the corridor in order to locate the ladder to the hold. As she passed by the base of the stairway to the upper deck, she saw through the open hatchway that it was nearly dawn. She had been awake longer than she thought. Surprisingly, someone else was already up and about. She heard footsteps on the deck approaching the stairs. Elissa turned, wondering who else had missed a night's sleep. It must be Favian! She was about to call a greeting, but stopped short when she realized that it was not just one set of boots but many tramping across the upper deck. Then she heard it, the tiny voice telling her, "Fly, fly away . . ."

Elissa ran back down the corridor and banged her fists upon her father's door with all her might. Within seconds the bar was lifted by the royal guards, their swords already in hand. Behind them she could see her father carrying a lamp.

"Hurry!" she cried. "Pirates!" But it was too late for warnings. Rough hands had already seized her from behind and dragged her back. Elissa struggled in vain. Before she could free herself, she felt the cold bite of steel against her neck.

"Put down your weapons." The voice that uttered the command from the shadows was no more than a whisper. Yet to Falk, holding the lamp at the entrance to his quarters, the words struck like blows directly to his heart. He gave

213

the signal to his guards. They handed their weapons to the intruders.

"You too."

Favian, who was attempting to creep unnoticed behind the pirates, reluctantly released his own sword and was pushed forward to stand with the guards.

One of the pirates stepped into the lamplight. Favian recognized the hideously scarred face in an instant and prepared himself for a confrontation.

"We meet again," said the one-eyed man in a hoarse whisper. However, he was not addressing Favian.

"I can't say it's a pleasure," Falk replied dryly.

"Oh, the pleasure is all mine," said Kreel. He turned to leer horribly at Elissa. "All mine."

# ❧ 12 ❧

# A Nightmare

Through a thin veil of dreams, Elissa heard a distant cry. The sound interrupted a conversation she had been having. Or perhaps she had only imagined she had been having a conversation. There was no one else in the cramped storage room where she had been confined since Kreel commandeered her father's ship. Yet she knew she had been talking to someone. A tiny voice had been whispering in her ear. It was saying something important.

"Who are you?" Elissa asked.

"Your moth—" it replied. Then the voice faded away.

"Where are they taking me?" Elissa asked. The voice may have answered her, but she could not remember what it said, for the cry had disrupted the fabric of her inner world, forcing her into partial wakefulness. She tried to reenter the dream, to ask again.

Since the night she had been locked into the dark hold of the ship, Elissa had retreated into the oblivion of slumber. For the most part, her dreams were a strange succession of disjointed images . . . Nana sitting by the fire, Gertrude clipping grass neatly with her teeth in a forest glade, a flock of white doves, an expanse of rainbow-hued flowers. These scenes comforted her. Sometimes, though, the images were grotesque . . . Kreel's misshapen grimace, the Khan's greasy fingers. She would awaken from these dreams terrified, only to pass into another dream . . . Om Chai chanting, or the little voice saying something important. But she could never remember what the moth had said when she awoke.

The cell possessed no porthole, so she had no idea whether it was day or night, and in the constant darkness there was no telling how long they had been traveling. By the count of her meals, perhaps ten days? She had been served ten times—stale hardtack accompanied by an unidentifiable slab of gray meat. The idea of consuming animal flesh revolted her, but after she had rejected the first few meals, her stomach hurt so dreadfully that she tried to eat some of the grisly mess. It was so tough, she could hardly chew it. She choked some of it down; the rest she threw into the crude privy that occupied one corner of her stinking cell.

In her half-awake state, Elissa couldn't help but wonder if any of this was real. Kreel's leering face, her gruesome cell, the little voice. Was it all a dream? A hallucination concocted by an over-wrought mind?

No, it was a nightmare. Elissa struggled to wake up.

The cry came again.

"Land ho!"

At last Elissa opened her eyes. This was the moment she had been dreading. For as long as the ship rocked and creaked, as long as she lay unconscious, she knew the inevitable encounter with Kreel would be delayed.

At the very thought of Kreel, the image of his contorted, scarred face rose up in her mind, mocking her. Elissa felt at fault for not having warned the others sooner. If Falk had known

Kreel was still alive, he might have been able to track him down. Unfortunately, she hadn't recognized Kreel at the Mermaid Inn. He had been sitting behind her, in the dark.

Darkness. If she could only see daylight. If she could only see Maya, Aesha, Gertrude, Favian—her father.

"Moth," she whispered, though she knew she would receive no answer. The only sound was the groaning of the anchor being lowered. Elissa sat up and ran her fingers through her hair. Over the past few months, it had grown into a mass of loose curls that tumbled down her back. She coiled it as best she could into a knot at the base of her neck. Then she shook out her cloak and smoothed it with her palms. She could not see herself, but she knew her clothes were filthy. She straightened her spine. The heavy thud of boots in the passageway was only a heartbeat away. Her time had indeed come.

The door to her cell creaked open. Before her stood a man holding a lantern. He spoke not a word to her, but his mission was obvious. Elissa thought briefly of running past him through the door, down the corridor, and up to the main deck . . . and then what? Would she dive overboard? It was a pointless plan. In any event, when she stood up, her legs barely supported her. She knew they wouldn't get her far. The man gestured for her to exit.

Once in the passageway, Elissa realized that any attempt at escape would have been futile, for three other men stood behind the door. They held short, effective-looking knives in their blunt fingers. In silence they marched her up the stairway to the main deck.

The sun was just setting as Elissa emerged into the world. She blinked, taking in the dimming sky with grateful eyes and eagerly inhaling the salt air with deep, hungry breaths.

"I trust you had a comfortable journey."

Elissa jumped. In the close confines of her cell, she had heard only the creaking of the ship and the occasional scrabbling of rats. The low rasp of the voice that broke the silence seemed to boom like a cannon.

Elissa turned to face Kreel. His face was hideous, but somehow it was less fearful in reality than it had been in her mind. She looked him directly in the eye. "Very," she replied evenly.

Kreel scowled. "You will be rejoining your companions shortly." He raised his hand, pointing an index finger toward the shore.

Following the direction of Kreel's gesture, Elissa gazed across the calm harbor. The landing was well protected, for the beach was backed by a set of sheer cliffs. As Elissa gazed upward, she realized the cliffs formed the foundation of a huge stone fortress. The structure rose seamlessly out of the dull gray rock, as cold and forbidding as the stone of which it was made. In the fog, she could not make out the top of the fortress.

*It's like the Citadel of the Khan,* she thought. *A mountain made by men.*

Upon the beach, a skiff was just landing. Elissa made out the small figure of Maya at the bow. Next to her sat Aesha, pale and tall. Beyond them, on the shore, stood a party of armed men surrounding her father and Favian. She counted them—four. Someone was missing.

"Where is my donkey?"

Kreel spread his lips cruelly. He waved toward the scullery, then rubbed his stomach suggestively.

"She was a tough old girl, but not so bad once

you got used to her," he said. Elissa could not take her horrified eyes from Kreel's hands as he slowly and deliberately unwound a leathery cord from his waist. It had a gray tassel at the end.

"Perhaps you would like a keepsake. It really doesn't work as a belt."

Elissa gagged. Before she could stop herself, she was leaning over the ship's railing. Kreel laughed as she retched.

"It's always nice to start the day with a good, lighthearted chuckle," he said.

A wave of fury washed over Elissa. But here—far from the green, growing things of the earth—there was no answering surge, no rush of Power. There was only rage. Screaming, she launched herself at Kreel. Then the darkness closed over her, sucking her into its depths, carrying her away.

Upon the shore, Falk stood anxiously, waiting for Elissa to land. From the moment she had been taken from him, he'd not had a moment's rest. It had been useless to offer gold, riches, land, or position to this twisted creature who was once a man. Kreel was mad, possessed. He held Elissa responsible for his disfigurement, for his exile, for his fall from grace. Nothing could distract him from exacting "justice" from her. Not even an exchange of victims.

"The Master will deal with you," was all he said when Falk had offered himself in exchange for Elissa. Whenever Falk pressed him for the name of his master, Kreel would contort his horrible face into what once might have been a smile. "You'll meet him soon enough."

As the boat carrying Elissa nudged against the sand, one of the pirates stepped forward to swing her to shore. He set her down on wobbly feet. To Falk she looked pale and thin, still not recovered from her trek up the mountain, but otherwise unharmed. It was clear she had not been allowed to bathe, yet she stood erect before him, her hair coiled and her cloak neatly pinned. As he stepped forward to grasp her by the shoulders, Falk breathed a sigh of relief. She had not been damaged physically. But when he looked into her eyes, he recoiled. Her eyes were like two chunks of ice—spiritless. Elissa looked right through him.

In a fury, Falk wheeled about to face Kreel. "What have you done to her?"

"Nothing." Kreel smirked. "Nothing at all."

Falk ground his teeth together. He drew Elissa close, near to his heart. He willed her to thaw, but she stood frozen in his arms. Something was trying to rise in his throat . . .

"You are my brave girl," he whispered in her ear. "More precious to me than all the riches of the world." The words were long overdue, but never had he felt them so strongly.

Falk felt a tremor. He had reached her, but when Kreel pulled her away from him, the emptiness in her eyes was almost more than he could bear. And still she did not speak. Falk would have given his kingdom to hear her utter a single word.

The group was ushered along the beach until they came to a set of stone steps cut directly into the rock. The fortress site was well chosen, for this narrow stairway, the only route to the top, would be easy to defend from an attack. *Whoever lives here must have many enemies*, Falk thought. As he watched Elissa climbing mechanically up the stairs ahead of him, he was grimly content to count himself as one of them.

They advanced in single file up the steeply angled steps, captives first. The prisoners had not been chained, as any attempt at escape would have been suicidal. Nevertheless, Favian was measuring the distance between steps, counting them, rehearsing possible attacks, assessing their chances, planning. Favian looked back over his shoulder. At the rear, a dozen or so men followed, carrying burlap sacks over their shoulders.

The group advanced up the gray steps in silence, saving their breaths for the climb. Occasionally Kreel broke out into an eerie high-pitched giggle, like a schoolboy who had just gotten away with a naughty prank. The stairway crawled relentlessly upward, occasionally doubling back upon itself like a coiled viper. They were allowed to rest on the shallow landings for only a few seconds.

Then, abruptly, the stairs ended.

They had reached the top. The group stood on a narrow stone ledge. Behind the ledge, the castle walls rose in a smooth, unbroken plane. Their arrival was expected, for a contingent of soldiers stood at the ready. Kreel stepped forward and spoke a few words to the captain of the guard, who merely nodded. The captain did not look at the prisoners as he led them away. Falk took Elissa's hand in his own. It lay there, cold and inert. She neither looked at him nor spoke.

Behind them, the sun's last rays glinted on the water, gathering in molten pools of gold. Two ships rested in the harbor, Falk's galleon and Kreel's dark pirate ship. There was no other land in sight.

"Get going." The guard's voice was so flat, he might have been speaking to himself.

The fortress loomed massive and forbidding before them. There were no windows. From the center of the structure rose a tower, its tip disappearing into the clouds. For sheer height, Falk had never seen anything like it. Nor would he ever expect to, for by all rights, this building shouldn't exist. The entire construction was an architectural impossibility. The walls were too massive to stand without a counterbalance. Moreover, the outer walls of the fortress actually leaned over them, yet there was no sign that they were anything but stable. It was as if they had been carved out of the living rock rather than erected.

The prisoners followed the guards to the entrance and, advancing single file under the raised portcullis, passed into a courtyard. There, another contingent of guards awaited them. Again Falk wondered who the lord of this island might be. For a man to command so great a fortress, with so many troops, and yet be unknown to Falk was an anomaly, for among lords, all of equal standing are either friend or foe. Wisdom dictates that a noble be able to distinguish, and deal with, each. A king must know them all by name.

They advanced into the fortress proper. Once inside they were led through a warren of dank, dimly lit corridors until they arrived at a pair of outsized doors.

"The Master is ready to see you," announced the guard.

The heavy doors slowly swung back to reveal a spacious room. In direct contrast to the rest of the fortress, the room was richly adorned. Tapestries depicting war exploits lined the walls. There were other exploits as well, horrifying in nature.

These were subtly woven into the borders. A pungent odor permeated the room. Faint at first, it might have been taken for a form of incense, though as they advanced farther into the room, the odor increasingly brought to mind the stench of a decomposing carcass. It appeared to be emanating from a huge, shapeless mass that occupied the far end of the chamber. In the dim light, it was difficult to make out its contours. It looked as though it might be an overstuffed couch of some sort, made perhaps of some hide that had been poorly cured. The guards pushed them forward, first Falk and Elissa—who seemed entirely unaware of her surroundings—then Favian, Aesha, and Maya. As they advanced, the stench grew steadily worse, until it was nearly overpowering. At the base of the couch, the group halted, looking to the left and to the right to determine which entrance the "Master" would choose. There appeared to be no doors—which left only one other possibility.

"Welcome." A subterranean voice rumbled from deep within the massed hides. Then the whole couch stirred.

The person—if that was what it could be

called—lying upon the dais was monstrous, so sunken in layers of flesh that it was nearly impossible to distinguish separate body parts. First a grossly misshapen arm rose from the mass, then the head. As the face took form, it became familiar. A wave of pure shame broke over Falk. This time he had failed both as King and as father.

"Welcome to World's End," said the Khan.

Maya shrieked and fainted dead away.

## ⤚ 13 ⤙

# World's End

As the prisoners entered the audience chamber, the Khan ran a moist pink tongue over his pendulous lips. This was the hour he had been awaiting. With greedy anticipation, he watched his captives approach—prolonging his victory, extending his triumph. King, Queen, Knight, a delicious little Pawn, and . . . could it be? . . . a delightfully pale Priestess. He had captured them all. Oh, how he enjoyed winning. These were the moments he lived for.

He felt a wave of pleasure at hearing the little Pawn shriek. This one would provide him with weeks, possibly months, of fun. But what had happened to the Queen? She hardly noticed his presence. He peered at her more closely. Gone was the vulnerable child he had once found so appealing.

Now she looked completely inaccessible—hard eyes, set jaw—just like her father. The Khan sighed in disappointment. Well, no matter. He had the little Pawn, the Knight, and the King. The Priestess looked interesting. Kreel had informed him that she might sing—with some persuasion. The Khan enjoyed persuasion. Ah, the mangled little spy had finally done well. He deserved a reward. Perhaps the Khan would give him the Queen.

The Khan gestured grandly. "Welcome to my humble abode," he said with a satisfied little smile. "Again."

The Khan was genuinely proud of his new fortress, though in all honesty, he could make no claim as to its construction. His pirates had come upon it some years ago—a formidable yet entirely deserted structure. There was no evidence of its former inhabitants. In fact, there was no mark of human presence at all, save the legend WORLD'S END carved over the stone archway of the entrance gate. Much of the time, you couldn't even make out the inscription. It was lost in the shadows cast by the immeasurably high walls of the central tower, the entrance to which neither he nor his men had yet discovered. He had made good use of the fortress. For it was here that he had stored his ill-gotten gains—plundered treasure, stolen goods, all the riches of the earth, which he had amassed strictly for the thrill of creating a deficit somewhere else. Unfortunately, his orgy of unmitigated greed had come to an abrupt end when he had been deposed.

The Khan frowned. *Barbarians!* Who would ever have suspected that those uncivilized Blue People would have been capable of organizing themselves against him! Not to mention his own mother! In the end, even she had betrayed him, drugging him into oblivion so that the tribes could rebel unimpeded. His deepest regret was that he'd not been able to catch her. The attack had been too sudden. His spies really should have informed him sooner. His spies should have informed him, period. He'd had to replace most of them, and nearly all his servants, which had reduced his network considerably. Not that it mattered. He was better suited to living here in this majestic keep, with his treasure close at hand, than wasting away in that boring desert. What's more, with the addition of his new armaments, he was guaranteed an unlimited supply of riches to come.

Ah, riches. Now that he had a weapon that would make him invincible, he would simply take it all: wealth, land, unlimited power. At first he had not believed it possible to harness the power of lightning. A single demonstration had convinced him that not only was it possible, but practical. There was no defense against it. With some work, the discovery might prove even more useful than its hapless inventor—foolish boy!— had imagined. Why, there was no limit to the ends to which the weapon might be put. Eventually, the Khan hoped to find a way to transform these simple black cylinders into massive instruments of destruction, weapons that could obliterate fortresses, armies, whole cities!

The Khan smiled. The thought of large-scale destruction was particularly pleasing to him, as it represented such an excess of suffering. He had been very clever at keeping the source of the black cylinders to himself. It was ironic, but somehow fitting, that the boy had been killed with his own weapon. Conveniently, he'd taken his brother with him, which suited the Khan well. Vengeful family members could be so inconvenient. Yes, the gods had smiled upon him once again. There was no doubt he was their favorite. Why, they might even make him one of them!

He would consider that eventually at greater length later, after he had entertained his visitors. Indeed, a King's ransom and some good, wholesome fun sounded like a delightful way to end his day. But the fun would come later. First he needed to make his little gaming pieces feel comfortable and secure. Afterward, he would destroy them, slowly, painfully—one by one. That was his special skill, one which had taken years of practice to perfect.

The group stood before him, waiting.

"But where are my manners?" cried the Khan. "You have not yet eaten, I trust? Perhaps you would like to freshen up before dinner?" He raised his hand, and half a dozen servants entered the room.

"Where are we, and what are your intentions?" demanded the young man.

The Knight was irritating. His manner was

entirely too self-confident for the Khan's taste. Well, that would be remedied soon enough.

"You are my guests," replied the Khan. "Nothing more." He placed a hand over his chest and addressed himself to the King. "I grow lonely here. I am desirous of interesting company, some pleasant chitchat to while the hours away, some . . . entertainment . . . to relieve my solitude."

He waited expectantly. The little Pawn, who had been revived but still trembled—most agreeably!—like a leaf, looked suitably alarmed, as did the tall Priestess. The Knight clutched at his side for an invisible sword. And the Queen looked . . . absent. It was the King's turn to move. The Khan was not disappointed.

"Thank you for the honor," the King said. "We would be most pleased to alleviate your boredom."

After the prisoners had been escorted from the room, the Khan settled himself contentedly into his cushions. It was almost time for him to move his first piece. The Game was about to begin.

☙ ❧

The ancient servant who escorted the girls to the women's quarters was a Blue tribeswoman. Maya wondered why the Khan had retained such an elderly maid. He normally preferred his servants young and malleable. This servant was so old, her face was withered like a prune and her fingers were bent and swollen at the joints. Maya thanked her politely, in the woman's own desert tongue, when they were delivered to their quarters. The old woman made no reply, scurrying back out through the door as if she were being chased. Maya felt a burst of sympathy for the poor old woman. All these years spent in the Khan's service must have been sheer torture.

After she had departed, Maya checked the door to the hallway. It was locked from the outside, of course. She sighed and settled herself on the divan. Later, more servants would arrive. There would be baths and new robes, followed by dinner, and then the Khan would begin to separate them. At all costs, they must remain together. She wanted to explain this to Elissa, but somehow her old friend had changed.

Something was terribly wrong with Elissa. She sat on a chair by the hearth, not seeming to care where she was. It was as though a vital part of her was missing. Aesha also sat quietly, on a small stool, staring at the wall. Or perhaps she was looking at nothing. Aesha often looked at nothing—pretty much all the time, in fact. But when Aesha looked at nothing, it seemed natural. Her eyes never seemed to focus. Unlike Aesha, Elissa always examined everything closely and carefully with those glowing eyes of hers. That was what had changed. Elissa's eyes no longer shone. They were as dull and lifeless as two pebbles.

Suddenly there was a grating sound, and the wall Aesha had been staring at opened.

"Good evening!" announced Favian cheerfully. He was crouched in a small gap near the floor.

Maya immediately jumped off the divan. "How did you find us?" she cried.

"I figured a fortress of this age would have many secret passageways," he said. "I found a suspicious-looking crack in the wall and tested it."

"Is the King with you?" asked Maya hopefully.

"No," replied Favian. "Regrettably, his rooms

are not connected to ours." He looked over to where Elissa was sitting. "How is she?" he murmured.

Maya shrugged. "She's not herself."

Favian stood up and immediately walked toward Elissa. He knelt down beside her chair and took her hand in his. It lay in his palm, unresponsive.

"Elissa," he said anxiously. "Can you hear me? Do you know who I am?"

Elissa said nothing, but she turned to look at him. Favian found himself gazing at a young woman who looked exactly like Elissa but, without her bright eyes and lively expression, somehow did not resemble Elissa at all. She looked at Favian as though he were a complete stranger.

"What did they do to you?" he whispered. She did not reply. Maya shook her head dismally.

Aesha, from her position at the center of the room, looked from Favian to Elissa to Maya.

"Have you noticed something?" she asked. The others had grown so accustomed to Aesha's silence that they jumped.

"The three of us," she continued, pointing

slowly at herself, Favian, and Maya. "Air, Fire, and Water." Maya and Favian looked at Aesha, then at one another as she pointed at them.

"You, Favian, are Fire. Maya is Water. I am Air," she explained.

Maya instantly bobbed her head up and down, saying in a bright voice that she'd known it all along. Favian looked perplexed, but gradually Aesha's meaning became clear to him.

"You're right," admitted Favian. He looked at Aesha and Maya thoughtfully, apparently coming to a decision: this was no time to withhold the truth. "Elissa knows I can make fire. And so, I believe, does Aesha."

Aesha nodded. Though she had said nothing, his feat on Wuayra Takiy had not escaped her attention.

"I can smell water," Maya announced.

Favian nodded. Somehow, he wasn't surprised. He had seen her swim. "Perhaps the three of us have come together for a reason," suggested Favian.

"Four," said Aesha, looking toward Elissa. "She is the one who brought us together."

"I'm not supposed to tell, but Elissa talks to

Gertrude," said Maya suddenly. She shrugged at Elissa, as if to offer apologies.

Favian looked down his nose at Maya. "I know *that*," he said. "Peasants"—he looked at Elissa—"I mean, *country people* talk to their animals nearly all the time."

"But Gertrude talks back," Maya insisted, piqued at his superior tone.

"Animals don't talk," replied Favian firmly.

"Oh, yes they do," argued Maya. "Elissa hears them. Camels tell jokes, bad ones, and they *really* like donkeys." Maya frowned. "Where *is* Gertrude, anyway?"

Favian was about to make a retort about Maya's poor grasp of animal husbandry when he heard an unusual wheezing sound coming from Aesha. It was such an odd noise, it took him a minute or two to identify what it was. Aesha was laughing.

"Fire and water," she breathed, "don't mix."

Favian looked down at little Maya, with her fists thrust adamantly against her hips, still insisting that animals told jokes, and he was tempted to laugh as well, until he noticed the moisture on Elissa's cheeks. She was crying. This was the first natural response she had made since landing on the island, though ironically it had been triggered by mention of that irritating donkey. Quickly Favian dropped to his knees before Elissa and placed his hands lightly but firmly upon her shoulders. He gazed into her eyes, searching for recognition. There was nothing, only a depthless pain that he could not identify, or soothe.

"Whatever we are meant to do," said Favian softly, "we will accomplish it together."

Elissa made no response, but Maya's face turned grave.

"As long as we do it far, far away from the Khan," she said fervently. She pointed to the secret passage, her voice urgent. "Go now, before the servant returns! If they discover you here . . ."

As Favian bent down to crawl through the secret passage, he cast a look back at Elissa. She hadn't stirred, but at least she was no longer crying.

# ☙ 14 ❧

# The Guest Room

Favian left the girls with not a moment to spare. No sooner had Maya pushed the tiny door shut behind him than the old servant returned bearing towels and robes. She attended to the girls efficiently, undressing, bathing, and dressing each of them in turn. She clothed Maya in a deep blue robe, the color of the South Sea. Elissa's gown was made of a forest-green velvet that hung in soft, clinging folds, perfectly complementing her eyes and skin—though Elissa donned it with such indifference, it might have been made of burlap. But when the servant touched the pouch that hung around Elissa's neck, Elissa clung to it with a fierceness that startled the old woman.

Aesha refused to put on the high-necked black robe the Khan had chosen for her, and wrapped the length of iridescent silk around herself instead. She reached up to pat Sweetheart, who was nestled comfortably in the cloth at the back of her neck. At the last moment, the old woman swept Elissa's hair into a high knot, securing it with Sohar's fibula. It was an act that left Maya puzzled. Surely the old woman, a desert tribeswoman herself, knew the fibula was not a hair ornament. And she surely must have recognized the distinctive markings of the Ankaa. But when they departed, Maya said nothing about the fibula, and merely thanked the woman warmly, which startled her. Thanks were a rare commodity in the Khan's fortress. A manservant stood beside their door, waiting.

Maya felt relieved that Favian had found his way to them. Even if they couldn't share the same quarters, they would at least be accessible to one another. She had to make the others understand that they must, at all costs, stay together. Maya knew all about the Khan and his little "games." He was not to be trusted, no matter how gracious he appeared to be at the moment. As they walked behind the manservant, Maya leaned toward Elissa.

"We must stay together," she whispered. She glanced at Elissa. Not a word had Elissa uttered since disembarking. Maya feared that her spirit had gone for good. She took Elissa's hand in hers. It was as cold as stone.

"Come back," Maya whispered.

The servant escorted them into a long, narrow dining hall. At the center of the room, a many-legged table blazed with hundreds of candles. Their flickering light danced on the walls but did not reach as high as the ceiling, an effect which produced the uncomfortable sensation that something might be lurking above them, hidden in the dark. Falk was already sitting at the far end of the table. As the girls approached, servants materialized from the shadows to pull chairs out for them. They sat in silence. Maya fidgeted in her seat anxiously, waiting for a servant to bring Favian. After a few moments, a houseboy appeared.

"The Khan regrets that he is unable to attend to you personally this evening. He had some unexpected business. He hopes that you will enjoy your repast." The houseboy waited, his face a perfect blank.

Maya, alarmed, jerked her head toward Falk. Falk motioned for her to keep still.

"Tell the Khan we look forward to dining with him tomorrow," he said calmly.

Falk and Aesha ate their dinners in silence, and without appetite, while Elissa sat perfectly still, leaving her food untouched. Maya pushed tiny bits of food around on her plate, trying to make it appear as though she were eating when in fact she could not, thinking that at this very moment the Khan had Favian in his clutches. The dinner stretched on interminably, course after course. At long last, tiny cups of tea were served, signaling the end of the meal, and moist, perfumed hand cloths were distributed on silver trays for the guests. A single manservant, the same one who had brought the girls to the dining hall earlier, appeared in order to escort the diners back to their rooms. Falk noticed the conspicuous lack of guards, but never doubted that a fully armed contingent of soldiers would materialize in an instant, should the need arise. He assumed they were being watched—and that the servant was armed.

They were escorted to Falk's suite first. At the

door, Falk turned and quietly announced that he would like to accompany the girls to their quarters in order to say good night to his daughter in private. The servant hesitated.

Falk stared into the man's eyes. "The Khan has promised us all due consideration and care," he said icily. "What is your name?"

Without a word, the servant led the group to the women's quarters. Once there, he allowed Falk to enter with Elissa, but he held his arm out to block Aesha and Maya.

"Just one at a time," he said.

"She hasn't been feeling well," said Maya. "It's a female problem."

The servant blushed slightly and indicated that Aesha and Maya might enter as well. He waited for Falk in the corridor, fidgeting with something in his pocket. The chambers only had one exit, so no one could escape. Nevertheless, he fingered the whistle in his pocket anxiously. One short blast would signal the rest of the guards. But that would make him appear incompetent, and the Khan punished incompetence severely. The guard shuddered. He decided to check the room.

He opened the door a crack and drew his knife. The outer room was empty. It appeared all four had entered the inner chambers. He swore under his breath.

The guard advanced through the anteroom and knocked softly on the door of the bedroom, like the humble servant he was supposed to be.

There was no answer. He pushed the door open. The tall woman stood smiling at him, her hair floating about her head like a white halo. Then the floor came crashing up and all was darkness.

"Where are you going?" Maya trotted alongside Falk, who, after disposing of the remnants of the shattered chair and dragging the guard into a closet, had led all of them down the hallway. Aesha held Elissa's arm, guiding her as one would guide a blind person.

"The Khan has probably thrown Favian into the dungeon," replied Falk. He searched the passage for a stairwell leading down.

"No," panted Maya. "He likes to do . . . things . . . in his private chambers."

Falk stopped in his tracks and looked at Maya. "Do you have any idea where . . . ?" he began.

He had no time to finish his question, for a figure stepped into the hallway in front of them. Falk tensed.

"Wait," said Maya. "I know her."

The servant beckoned to them. Then she spoke in a guttural language that only Maya understood.

"She is going to lead us to Favian," said Maya.

Falk regarded Maya skeptically. "How do you know what she intends to do? We could be walking into a trap."

Maya tugged at Falk's sleeve impatiently. "We must follow her," she insisted. Falk did not have a chance to reply, for Maya had grabbed Elissa's lifeless hand and was already following the old woman, with Aesha close behind. For an aged servant, the old woman moved with surprising speed down the long, dark corridor. When they came to a junction, the old woman halted and indicated a passageway to their right. She spoke to Maya in clipped, breathless whispers.

"The Khan keeps his Special Guests here," translated Maya. "The Guest Room adjoins his quarters. It is locked from the outside. There are no windows, so escape is impossible." The old woman waved her hand toward the passageway in a gesture that needed no translation: *Go quickly. Before it is too late.*"

Maya peered up into the woman's face. "Thank you, grandmother," she whispered.

The old woman made a stifled noise, like a dry little sob. "I only twenty-five," she said in halting Common Tongue. "One winter past, I Special Guest of Khan." Then, before anyone could say a word to her, she ran down the hallway.

Maya gasped and started after her, but Falk held her arm.

"It's too late for her," he said. "Let's go before it's too late for Favian."

Maya led the group down the hallway to a small door. As the servant had said, it was locked. Falk sighed in frustration.

"We can't get in this way," he said.

Maya was turning her head, gazing down the dim corridor. "She said that the Khan's quarters are down there and to the right," she said, pointing. "I don't think we should get any closer."

Falk followed the direction of Maya's finger

and nodded. "You two take Elissa and go back to my quarters. Wait for me there. I will stay and create a distraction to force the Khan from his chambers. While the guards are searching the corridor, I will find the connection to the Guest Room."

Maya crossed her arms over her chest.

"*Go!*" he repeated, as forcefully as he could without raising his voice. "It's the only way to free Favian."

"We mustn't separate," protested Maya. "It's dangerous. The Khan will pick us off one by one, and then how will we rescue Favian? He'll *die*."

Elissa had stood silently throughout the exchange. She heard voices, as if from a great distance. Occasionally a word drifted through the fog—*the Khan . . . Favian . . . die*. An awareness of their situation slowly penetrated her dulled senses. Her father was about to do something dangerous. Favian was going to *die*. Suddenly, the mists that had shrouded Elissa's mind cleared. She stepped forward and, reaching up to remove the fibula from her hair, crouched down to examine the lock.

The lock was large but not complex.

*Showy, but useless,* thought Elissa. *Just like the Khan.* It only took a few seconds for her to locate the catch. An unconscious smile of satisfaction flickered over Elissa's lips, as it always did whenever she heard a lock release. Falk helped Elissa to her feet, gazing into her face with profound relief, while Maya hugged her tightly.

"You're back!" Maya cried.

Elissa *was* back. She didn't reply, but the smile she gave Maya was genuine, if brief.

"We don't have long," warned Maya, though looking into Elissa's sad but once again bright eyes, she could not help but smile as well. Falk and Elissa entered the room, leaving Aesha and Maya to stand guard at the door.

Although the Guest Room was dimly lit, Elissa could see that it was spacious, and littered with instruments and tools. There was an odd, bed-shaped platform at the center, but lacking curtains, mattress, and bedding, it didn't look much like a place where one could sleep. Behind the platform was a wide doorway, undoubtedly leading to the Khan's quarters. They advanced cautiously into the room.

Inside, the stench was unbearable. Elissa

identified it as the smell that the Khan's bloated body produced. It was the odor of rot. And fear. There was also the smell of something burnt. A low moaning came from the far corner of the room.

*Favian!*

Elissa rushed forward.

Favian uncurled himself from the pile of rags where he had been lying. His clothing was torn to shreds. On closer inspection, Elissa could see it was singed.

"Oh!" he said. "It's you!" He smiled gloriously. "I thought it was Fatso."

Elissa leaned over Favian, inspecting his face for bruises. "Are you hurt?" she whispered.

"No." He whispered low into Elissa's ear. "Hot coals and brands. I'm fine, but he's ruined my shirt." Favian plucked at the tattered black silk. "It was my *best* shirt, too," he muttered. Elissa took him by the arm, and Favian rose easily to his feet and bowed to Falk, who, having his eye on the door to the corridor, had missed their exchange.

"I think the Khan is asleep," Favian said in a low voice. "But we had better hurry, in case he wakes up and decides to check on my . . . welfare." Favian accompanied Elissa and Falk to the door, but touching his hip, he hesitated. "Wait, he's got my sword. I'd better go back."

Falk grasped him by the shoulder. "You want to return to that den of horrors?"

"I can't leave my sword," Favian said stubbornly.

"Remarkable," murmured Falk, with obvious admiration.

"We've got to get out of here now!" Maya hissed. "The Khan is *right . . . there.*" She jabbed her finger urgently toward the Khan's chambers.

The group moved down the hallway, Falk in the lead. Miraculously, it was still deserted.

"The Khan doesn't like to be disturbed from his slumber," whispered Maya. "So nobody dares come near him when he's sleeping."

Falk stopped and faced Favian, who somehow had become second in command. "We should try to get back to the beach," said Falk. "The ship is our only hope."

Favian nodded. "Unless we grow wings and fly," he said softly, casting a meaningful glance at Elissa.

Elissa smiled at their private joke, remembering how irritating she had once found that suggestion. When Falk turned away, Favian leaned close to Elissa. "We missed you," he murmured. Favian had no idea what had happened to Elissa on the ship, but he made a silent promise to make it right, especially if that task involved killing Kreel.

They soon came to the end of the hallway. A gate led out to the courtyard, which was already filling with guards.

Falk held out his hand to hold them back. "It seems word of our escape has spread. We'll have to find another way out," he said.

The group backtracked through the looping corridors, hoping to find another exit, but each hallway led them straight back to the central courtyard. The guards were dividing into groups for the search. It wouldn't be long before they were discovered.

"We haven't gone down this one yet," said Maya.

She pointed at a dark, narrow passageway.

"It might be a dead end," said Favian.

They could hear the guards shouting orders.

"We don't have a choice," Falk said, pushing Favian and the others forward. As they ran down the passageway, Favian prayed out loud for a door.

He got his wish.

At the end of the passage was a wide wooden door. Surprisingly, it wasn't locked. Favian pushed it open and they all piled inside. Once the door was shut, they found themselves plunged into total darkness. Nobody dared take a step for fear of falling off a ledge or down a shaft. Favian turned his back to the group and held up his hand. In a moment a faint glow was cast over a large workroom.

He let out a low whistle. "Well, what have we here?"

The room was filled with black cylinders of every dimension. They ranged from hand-sized to cylinders large enough to crawl into. They were heaped on the floor, stacked against workbenches and high stools. Scattered about on the tables were tools of all sorts—lathes, files, wheels. And against the far wall were piles and piles of burlap sacks.

Falk had moved ahead of Favian to survey the

room. "I believe it's an assembly room for that weapon you showed me," he said. "There are probably others, and metalworks, of course." Favian leaned over the sacks, examining their contents.

"Careful with that candle," warned Falk. "There is enough weaponry in this room to destroy the entire island."

*The whole world*, thought Elissa. She envisioned the destruction she had witnessed in the jungle multiplied a thousand times, for there were thousands of weapons in this room. And in the hands of the Khan . . . Elissa shuddered at the thought.

The sound of distant shouts came through the door.

Favian felt around among the cylinders with his free hand until he found one that fit into his palm.

Falk shook his head. "They're probably empty," he said. "Most of these weapons don't look even half finished."

"Yes, but we can use them as cudgels."

Falk nodded. "I like your thinking," he said. Favian and Falk began rummaging around for more cylinders.

"Wait!" Aesha was examining the wall behind a workbench, running her fingers along a tiny crack in the wall. Her hair was floating about her head in a curious fashion.

"Look," she said. "There is an air current here." She pointed at something none of the rest of them could see. Aesha pressed against the crack. It made a creaking noise, and then a door sprang open. Behind the opening was a narrow chamber.

"We can at least hide in there for a while," said Favian. "That will win us a little time to come up with a good strategy."

"If we have more time, so do they," said Falk, but the sound of heavy boots tramping down the hallway convinced him. In a flash, all five of them squeezed through the opening. They pushed at the door, which slid back into place, blending back into the wall invisibly. From the outside there would be not a trace of where they had gone. Once again, they found themselves in pitch-blackness.

"Where's the light?" asked Falk.

"Right here," said Favian.

A little light sprang up. Favian advanced and

raised his hand so the others could see. Above them, a narrow set of circular stairs wound as far as the light could reach.

"Clever of you to have brought that candle," said Falk approvingly.

Favian did not reply, but Elissa stepped close behind him, blocking his hand from Falk's view.

Aesha raised her head. "The air is flowing up. There is an opening at the top."

As she looked up into the darkness, Elissa had the distinct sensation that something up there was waiting for her. The sensation was so strong, it was almost as if she heard her name being called.

Elissa set her foot on the first stair, but Favian held her back.

"Allow me," he said. He looked toward Falk for permission to lead.

"You have the light," Falk said, waving his hand.

Favian led the group up the stairs, holding his hand up high. Elissa, Maya, and Aesha followed close behind. Falk brought up the rear.

Cautiously at first, the group began to climb the winding stairs. Like the steps that had been carved into the cliff by the beach, the stone stairway seemed to ascend forever, and if not for the little light Favian held before him, they would have been compelled to make the climb in total darkness. There were no windows. As they made their way up the winding stairway, it became clear they were climbing the central tower. They stopped from time to time to rest their weary legs. At no point did they pass a door or any kind of opening.

Favian held his little light up, examining the stones on either side of the stairway for telltale cracks. But the rocks fit together so tightly, a hair wouldn't pass between them.

"Wonderful work," murmured Falk. "Whoever built this fortress was a master craftsman."

*Is,* thought Elissa. Even though the fortress exuded an aura of impenetrable age, she knew its maker was still alive. She also knew that whoever had made it was waiting for them at the top of the stairs. *The end of the world is near,* she thought.

The group stopped to catch their breaths and stretch their calves.

"We are not being followed," said Falk, look-ing back.

"All well and good," said Favian. "But I am beginning to think this tower goes to heaven."

"The stairs will come to an end soon," said Aesha. Again she pointed in front of her, at something invisible. Aesha made a spiraling mo-tion with her hand. Her silk sleeve fluttered slightly.

Aesha's gesture motivated them all to pick up their pace. Soon, just as Aesha had predicted, they came upon a door. It was slightly ajar.

"Can you see inside?" asked Falk, beginning to push past the others.

Favian shook his head. "By your leave, sire," he said. "I'll go in first."

Falk hesitated for an instant. Favian's hand, holding up the light, remained steady. Falk nod-ded.

Cautiously, Favian pushed open the door and passed through. He held up his hand.

The room at the top of the tower appeared to be perfectly round, the walls curving smoothly inward to form a high dome. The center of the room was occupied by a large circular hearth that glowed with a faint light. Favian lifted his hand higher to illuminate the far reaches of the room. It seemed that someone, or some*thing*, was waiting for them. A shadowy form was perched upon a stool beside the hearth. Motioning Elissa and the others to stay back, Favian advanced, one hand held high, the other feeling for the weapon that no longer lay against his hip. Slowly, the figure rose. To his utter surprise, it was a tiny woman.

Elissa came up from behind him until she, too, could see into the room. Then she let out a little gasp. She started forward.

"Not again," Favian groaned. "Somebody stop her!" He reached out his free hand, only to clutch at emptiness. Elissa had eluded his grasp. She ran into the room, holding out both hands as if greeting a long-lost friend.

"Nana!" cried Elissa. "What on earth are you doing here?"

"This is where I live," replied Nana calmly. "Now come in, everyone, and have some tea."

# ⮞ 15 ⮜

# The Phoenix

The Ancient One sat upon her three-legged stool, surveying the little group with a keen eye. The Seeker had done well. The Ancient One tipped her head in Elissa's direction. The girl was sniffing suspiciously at her tea.

"What does she think is in there? Poison?" mumbled the Ancient One. She moved her gaze to the rest of the group. Beside Elissa crouched Water, seeking the low point. Wind stood at a slight distance from the rest, holding her cup but not drinking from it. The Windsinger's eyes soared upward, toward the top of the domed ceiling, toward freedom. The Ancient One nodded and smiled. Wind would play her part well when the time came.

Fire was peering into the dark recesses of the

room, trying to find an escape route. *Hee-hee,* she cackled to herself. *He won't find one.* Every once in a while, his hand strayed to his hip. They were all here, all accounted for. She even had one extra, for luck—or not, as the case might be. Luck could flow in either direction.

Falk stood behind Elissa. The man had changed since the Ancient One had last seen him. A door had opened in his heart. She hadn't counted on this kind of complication. He might pose a problem. But life was full of little surprises, and time was running short. Her task was at hand. The Ancient One cleared her throat.

"I suppose you must be wondering why I have gathered you all here," she said. That got their attention.

"*You* . . . gathered *us?*" Hands on hips, Favian posed the challenge. She had expected that.

"Yes, indeed," she said equably. "Or, to be more correct, Elissa did. However, I was the one who sent her after you." The Ancient One rose from her stool and approached Favian.

"Fire," she said, taking his hands into her own. "Welcome." His hands were warm. She let them go, and then turned to Aesha and took the Windsinger's hands, insubstantial and light.

"Wind, don't be afraid. Welcome to my home."

"Nana." Elissa spoke gently. "This isn't your home. You live in High Crossing."

"For a time, yes, I made my home there. I have had so many. But this was one of my first."

"This fortress is yours?" Elissa frowned and blinked. She knew Nana better than to question her. Nevertheless, Nana as mistress of a fortress was a hard concept to swallow.

"It was, until the Khan took it over. He always manages to move into my best houses," the Ancient One said. "He's worse than a cowbird."

Falk stepped forward with authority, attempting to take control of a situation that was veering toward chaos. "You've gone mad, Nana," said Falk firmly. "Kreel brought us here, not Elissa. And this business with the Khan has absolutely nothing to do with you."

Favian was rubbing his forehead and squinting, like a man with an intolerable headache. "You know her, too?" he asked Falk.

"Of course. She was Elissa's guardian," replied Falk.

"But why is she *here*?" Favian looked from Falk to Nana and back again, as if sensing an old collusion, a secret, something kept from him.

"I've been trying to tell you," said the Ancient One irritably. "I have a task for you." She turned to Falk. "Stand back, my lord. You were not expected. Just the five."

Elissa gasped in pain. Her fifth companion had not made it.

"Oh, Nana . . ." Elissa couldn't contain her sorrow any longer. She put her arms around the old woman and wept.

"No need for that," said the Ancient One. "You've nothing to cry about."

"Oh, but Nana," sobbed Elissa. "Gertrude . . . they made me, made me—"

"Made you what?" asked Gertrude, stepping out of the shadows.

"Gertrude!" cried Elissa. "You're alive!"

"Of course I am," huffed the donkey. "Not that *you* had anything to do with it."

"What happened?" Elissa was dumbfounded.

"Well, that nasty cook came at me with a

carving knife. I knocked a few of his teeth out, but he still got part of my tail. Nobody came near me after that. So when the boat finally stopped heaving around, I kicked the stall apart, jumped off, and swam to shore. The Old Lady found me and fixed up my tail." She swished a shorter but complete tail. "She's pretty good at fixing things."

Gertrude nodded her head in Nana's direction. The old woman reached into her robe and drew out something small and shiny—a tin of heal-all.

"This was for you to *keep*," she said accusingly. "Not to give away. You think making this stuff is easy?"

Elissa's eyes were fixed on the tin in total disbelief. "You mean that was *your* cottage in the woods?" It seemed an age ago since she had taken refuge in the hermit's cottage in the glade. It *was* an age ago.

"I told you I had many houses." Nana was getting annoyed with all this talk. "But this is no time to discuss architecture! We have to get on with it!" The old woman was practically hopping with impatience.

But Elissa had thrown her arms around Gertrude's neck, temporarily deaf to the world.

"I'm so glad I didn't eat you," she murmured into the donkey's ear.

"What?" brayed Gertrude.

Falk started, his eyes bulging. "She's speaking!" he cried.

Elissa turned to her father, chagrined. He must have been so worried. "Oh, I am sorry I've been so distant. You see, I thought . . ."

"No, the donkey! She can talk." Falk's mouth was hanging open in pure amazement.

"See?" said Maya, nudging Favian. "I told you!"

The old woman advanced purposefully toward Falk. Her patience had finally run out. "You are standing on Elissa's locus!" She jerked her arm out and pointed at Falk's feet.

"Her . . . *what?*" Falk looked down. Under his feet lay a circular green stone. It shone unlike any stone he had ever seen. From deep within, it glowed like an immense emerald—like Elissa's eyes.

Nana was pushing him off the stone. "You understand Gertrude because you are standing on Elissa's *spot*. Now get off," she said. "Come, all the rest of you." She pushed Falk back, away from the group.

The Ancient One turned toward the others, shaking her head. There was no use explaining anything to these simpletons. They had no sense of priorities, and besides, her time had run out. Favian was still squinting; he opened his mouth . . .

"Hush!" The Ancient One lifted her arm. Her sleeve fell back as she raised it, revealing a long, bony protrusion tipped with five claws. Seen in their true context, those claws could never be called fingers. Nor could the protrusion properly be called an arm. The effect was galvanizing. Everyone held perfectly still. When she re-adjusted her sleeve, five sets of eyes followed the movement in perfect silence.

Drawing their eyes downward, the Ancient One pointed to the stone floor, forcing them to finally take notice of what lay beneath their feet. There, set into the stone floor around the hearth, were five stone circles: the green stone that Falk had inadvertently stepped on and four others. Slowly, deliberately, the Ancient One pointed from one stone to another, and as she pointed, each circle began to glow.

"Now we must begin," she pronounced. "Take your places."

"Begin what?" asked Elissa. She had an awful premonition.

The Ancient One looked at her with eyes that did not blink.

"You never did listen to me," she said. "I've been telling you for years. I am the Phoenix."

"Those stories . . . ," said Elissa. She'd thought they were just tales.

The Ancient One nodded. "Now it is time for me to die."

Elissa reached out, as if she could hold the old woman back from her trajectory toward oblivion. But the Ancient One drew away from Elissa's outstretched fingers. "It's no use trying to prevent it, child. If I don't die, the rest of you will."

"What do you mean?" Elissa looked wildly around at the group—Maya, Aesha, Favian, Falk, Gertrude. "Do you mean us?"

The Ancient One snorted in disgust. "No, not just you—your little selves, your little bodies, your puny little lives. *All of you!*" The Ancient One fixed her glittering black eyes on Elissa. "I think you know what I mean," she said.

And, gazing into Nana's eyes, Elissa did. Everything suddenly fit together: the advancing desert, the drying swamp, the crop-killing frosts. "You mean the drought?" she said cautiously.

The Ancient One cocked her head to one side. "That, and more." Her voice was remote, cold. "Much more. More than you can imagine."

Elissa felt a chill creep up her spine. "The prophecy." A tremor crept into her voice. "It's the end of the world, isn't it?" What she didn't understand, had never understood, was about to be made clear. And suddenly she had no desire to unravel the mystery, to see it for what it was, for she already knew the face of death, and hated it.

The old woman's lips twisted into an odd little smile. "Not to fear, child," she said. "Not to fear."

Elissa tried to calm the trembling in her knees. Nana hadn't changed at all—she still explained nothing—but now Elissa believed that all those years of silent watching and waiting were a blessing in disguise. She didn't want to know what was in Nana's mind.

The old woman had turned her back to Elissa

and made her way across the room. When she stood facing Maya, she merely said, "It's time."

As was her way, Maya seemed to understand, for when the Ancient One took her by the hand and led her to the closest circle, she went willingly. As she approached the stone, it glowed with a clear blue light.

"Stand here," commanded the Ancient One.

Maya inhaled deeply. She could smell the great pool of liquid that lay far beneath her feet. It called to her. It spoke of fathomless depths, of silence, and of home. There was no question that she belonged right where she stood. As she placed her small feet upon the stone, she heaved a deep sigh of pleasure and recognition. "Mother!" she said.

The Ancient One turned away, seeking the next one. "Wind!" she called. Aesha was already moving toward her locus, transfixed by the light. The circle lying at her feet matched her eyes. It swirled in ever-changing patterns. It was movement, song, the breath of life.

"Hanan Pacha," Aesha said, laughing softly. *Sky*. As her feet touched the locus, an updraft seemed to rise from the stone, causing the pale silk gown to billow around her, disturbing both her hair and the small gray bird resting on her shoulder.

As Aesha lifted her hand to soothe Sweetheart, the Ancient One made an abrupt gesture, and a flutter of wings signaled Sweetheart's flight. The bird came to rest on Gertrude's head. Aesha turned to find him.

"He'll be safer there," the Ancient One reassured Aesha, but even as she spoke, she was moving away, toward the next Element. The task was now close at hand, and her body was craving heat.

"Fire, would you do me the honor?" The Ancient One pointed to her cooling hearth.

Implicitly, Favian understood what was expected of him. "Of course," he said. Favian stepped forward and clapped his hands over the hearth. A second later, the entire bottom of the hearth blazed up as the smoldering coals reignited. The light from the coals cast flickering shadows over an object that lay nestled in the center of the hearth. It looked very much like an overturned terra-cotta soup pot to Elissa—a broken one at that. There was a jagged hole at the top.

"You may take your place now," said the Ancient One. Favian made his way directly to a deep red stone the color of garnet, with as little resistance as had Maya and Aesha. For just as they had felt the call of their Elements, so had he felt the fire contained within the glowing stone. His whole body tingled. Unconsciously, he touched his hip.

"Oh, I almost forgot," said the Ancient One. She clucked to herself and withdrew a sword from her robe. "I believe this is yours."

Favian took his sword gratefully from her hands, though his eyebrows were raised inquiringly.

"I have my ways," she said, smiling. "After all, I built this place. Nobody knows it as I do."

There was one person left, the most important one of them all: the Seeker. The old woman turned away from Fire, and approached Elissa. Taking up both her hands, she looked into the girl's face.

"I raised you, trained you, and sent you into the World." The Ancient One looked deeply into Elissa's eyes. "And don't you ever forget it." Her gaze was steady, unblinking, and not focused on

Elissa at all, for she was seeing something not contained in any mortal face. Perhaps she was looking into the future, but what she saw there, she would not tell.

Bravely, Elissa returned that inhuman gaze. As she looked into the Ancient One's eyes, she saw the gateway to the past. It was like looking down into a bottomless well, the march of countless years receding forever, into blackness, into nothing—until they met the future. She knew that what she was seeing was Eternity, and that she could not grasp it. No human could.

For a timeless moment, Elissa hung breathless, suspended in the infinite space between heaven and earth. Then the vision slipped away, as does a dream. And there was only Nana, standing before her, tiny and frail.

At last Elissa understood. And she despaired of that knowledge.

"Will you still remember us . . . afterward?" she said.

Nana shook her head slowly. "No, my dear."

"Not even me?" Elissa's voice was sharper than she had intended. Nana sighed. "This is the purpose for which you were born, child. I am

273

sorry if I have used you, but, you see, there really was no other way. It was up to you to find the Others, for you are the one who binds them all together."

The old woman took Elissa's hand and led her to the green circle. Elissa's legs moved reluctantly, as if they were made of wood.

"Take your place."

Elissa walked toward the stone. She had no choice but to obey Nana's command, no matter what the outcome. But hadn't it been that way all along? Nana had always directed her actions. Elissa desperately wanted to cry out against the Fates. She felt cheated. Death had robbed Elissa of her mother so long ago, she could not even remember her face. And now it was going to take away Nana as well. The worst part was that Nana had known all along that it was going to turn out this way—because she had planned it.

Elissa took her place with a heavy heart, feeling the cruelty of Om Chai's prophecy in her bones. But as she stepped upon the glowing green stone, a wave washed over her, knocking all thought from her mind. The shock was so powerful that she swayed slightly with the impact.

The Power coursed up her spine and through her body, stronger than it had ever been—stronger than it had been in the desert, stronger than it had been in the jungle. Now it was taking her with it, carrying her away. Elissa tried to resist. She struggled for control, for mastery.

"Let it happen," said Nana softly.

Elissa closed her eyes and obeyed. She relinquished herself, and with that surrender came a profound sense of recognition. She felt the warmth of the earth; the movement of living things; the moist richness of vegetation, growth, abundance, fertility. She smelled the sweet, heavy odor of the jungle flower that only bloomed at night, Erda's bloom. She felt the serene stillness of the hermit's forest glade, where the trees had told her their secret—that from the tiniest bud to the strongest trunk, from the loftiest branch to the deepest root, the forest was a single interwoven entity, as were the earth that nourished it and the beasts that inhabited it. And all of it— the sounds, scents, and sights of the Earth— resonated deep within her in a steady thrum—the song of the Earth. Her song.

"Do you know who you are now?"

Elissa smiled at the old woman she had known as Nana, realizing that she had never really understood anything until now. "Yes," said Elissa, smiling. She was whole at last—at peace.

"Nothing else matters," said the Ancient One. She stood, waiting. "Give it to me now," she said.

Elissa did not have to be told what the Ancient One wanted.

The girl drew the velvet pouch from her bodice, where it had lain next to her heart all these months, and emptied the shard into her palm.

The Ancient One shook her head. "Spendthrift," she muttered, plucking the shard lightly from Elissa's outstretched hand. "What on earth did you do with all that gold?" But she looked pleased. "I forgot to pick up this piece last time," she explained.

Then she reached out and, casually passing her hand through the flames, placed the shard upon the pot, where it fit perfectly into the uneven hole. The pattern was now complete. The shard's indecipherable wavy lines, the ones that had plagued Elissa—so familiar, yet so unreadable—became mountains opening onto a high valley where paths crossed. A thin river lay between them, threading its way south. Elissa recognized her home in an instant. High Crossing was the missing piece! Suddenly the whole sphere blazed a deep green. It turned, revealing its bright hues. Turquoise, jade, and moss. Emerald, malachite, and mint. Rugged mountains and rough deserts; silken lakes; flowing rivers and streams; the steady inhalation and exhalation of the sea—all revolving before them in an endless knot of interweaving designs.

"It's round!" whispered Elissa excitedly. "The earth is round! I knew it!"

"Anybody with a little wingspan could have told you that," remarked the Ancient One. "Now be quiet. The pentagram is almost complete."

Elissa looked down. Between the stones, five glowing lines had formed, making a five-pointed star, the hearth at its center. Four stones were occupied, but there was still one empty locus—a circle as white as the summit of Wuayra Takiy. The last element had yet to be represented: Spirit.

Elissa looked at Gertrude, and at Falk. Neither one had been allowed to enter the pentagram. "Who is the fifth?" Elissa asked quietly.

The Ancient One did not answer. "Stay where you are," she said. "No matter what happens, no matter what you see, *don't move*. None of you!" Then she reached out to snatch something that flitted by Elissa's ear.

"No!" the girl cried, but it was already too late. Before Elissa could stop her, the Ancient One had crushed the moth within her withered claw. Tears glittered in Elissa's eyes. The little being who had guided her, warned her, protected her, was no more.

"It was harmless," Elissa whispered. But the old woman did not hear, or, if she did, she gave no acknowledgment. She was walking slowly, stiffly, to the fifth circle. There, the Ancient One extended her hand above the stone and released the broken wings of the moth. They drifted downward, two insignificant motes of pale dust.

"How *could* you?" Elissa's voice was thick with reproach.

The Ancient One ignored Elissa's accusation. At this point she did not have the time to explain herself, and soon, very soon, the answer would be obvious. So she simply stood beside the stone, shaking the dust from the moth's tiny wings from her sleeve. The dust fell so slowly, it seemed suspended. Then, almost imperceptibly, it began to swirl in a loose, winding helix.

Without bothering to watch the drifting debris from that small death, the Ancient One turned and made her way back to the hearth. Her time had come, and nothing else mattered.

Once she reached the hearth, she turned, raising her arm in an abrupt gesture. "Sing!" she commanded, pointing at Aesha.

Aesha looked at the Ancient One, helpless. But then, as Aesha's throat filled and swelled with the beginnings of the Song, her mouth opened. A sound like nothing on earth came forth. It echoed through the room, rebounding off the walls, meeting itself on its return. She sang two notes at once; three, four, a whole chorus. The intervals spiraled downward and then upward again, like the ebb and flow of the wind.

"Come!" sang Wind. "Come to us!" And as she sang her invitation, the air began to move. The flames spat and hissed in the hearth. Fanned by the moving air, the heat from the hearth mounted.

Fire leaned closer. He glanced down at his

279

sword handle. It glowed. So did his hand. In fact, all of him was glowing. His whole body was crackling with an energy he could barely contain. In an excess of sheer exhuberance, Fire laughed out loud. He looked toward the others, wondering if they, too, felt this strong, this vital.

Water shimmered slightly and then began to melt, though she didn't diminish in size. She seemed to be flowing. Her limbs and dress were merging together, fusing into a single form, melding into the stone that lay beneath her. It was hard to make out her face, but Water was smiling.

Now Wind was losing her form as well. She was becoming sheer movement. Her hair, which normally floated lightly about her head, was whirling rapidly. The pale silk dress whipped and snapped violently about her with increasing strength. And yet she sang—the Song pouring out of her throat, out of her entire being.

Earth had turned bright green, all of her—feet, hands, face—right up to the hair on her head. And, wonder of wonders, she was blossoming. Around her head, a row of waxy white blooms opened, circling her hair like a crown.

The sweet scent of a jungle night wafted through the air. Her eyes, always large, were huge. They were filled with joy.

And, last of all, over the snow-white stone, a figure was solidifying. Gradually, like a half-forgotten dream, or a suppressed memory coming to the surface of consciousness, a young woman as translucent and ephemeral as smoke took form. She was so beautiful, it hurt to look at her. There was a purity of spirit in her face that mortal eyes were never meant to see. Spirit lifted up her chin to gaze at Earth, to meet Earth's green eyes with her own. She smiled—the infinitely tender smile that only a mother can give.

Falk could bear it no longer. A single word burst forth from his lips: "Galantha!" He took a step forward.

"Keep still!" cried the Ancient One. Falk stood still, as she commanded, but he reached out his hands to grasp the apparition, to hold her fast to him. Gertrude stepped forward and blocked Falk, backing him gently away.

At that moment, the fire blazed up to cover the sphere. Its immense heat could be felt in the farthest recesses of the room. With a cry of triumph, the Ancient One threw herself into the hearth. The flames grew higher and brighter as, with a great roar, they consumed her. Their blinding light filled the room. Fire's hand strayed to his sword. This time he grasped it and drew it from its sheath. It glowed red in his hand; flames licked along its edge. And all around him, Aesha's Song rang with the wind, a wind that howled as the flames rose to meet the top of the domed ceiling. Grasping the handle with both hands, he held his sword straight up over his head.

The bolt that split the top of the dome could have fallen from the sky or risen from the sword—they would never know for certain. The only thing they could be sure of was that the roof was shattered—along with the sphere. And from its remains rose the Phoenix, stretching her golden beak, her rainbow-hued wings, to the sky. She rose in a glorious symphony of light, brighter than the Fire from which she had emerged. As the Phoenix rose, a sweet, fragrant rain fell softly upon the hearth, dampening the flames. Gradually the flames receded, leaving behind a bed of cooling embers. And of the sphere, only its scattered pieces remained.

Slowly, majestically, the Phoenix continued to rise from the hearth, embers falling from her wings in a sparkling cascade. Then, as if suddenly breaking free from an invisible bond, she flew straight up, through the broken roof. She hovered above them for a moment. And then, with a single clap of her brilliant wings, she was gone.

When the second bolt hit, they were still gazing upward, their damp faces lifted heavenward toward the countless shining embers that filled the deep velvet dome of the sky.

## ✥ 16 ✥

# The Beginning

Something had disturbed the Khan's slumber. He shifted uneasily, trying to readjust the soothing mantle of sleep, but when the second clap of thunder knocked him to the floor, he was jolted awake with firm finality. This disruption of his otherwise entertaining evening was unconscionable, unforgivable. Once he located the culprit, there would be retribution. Not only had his beauty sleep been interrupted, but most unpardonable of all was the fact that once his enormous bulk was anchored to the floor, he could not get up. To make matters worse, the servants' bell was out of reach. It was next to the bed, not next to the floor. He shouted for assistance, but not one of his servants heard him. The Khan's private chambers were heavily insulated against sound. The songs he extracted from his victims were for his ears alone.

The Khan shouted until he became hoarse. Then he lay still. The carpet was thick. Nevertheless he could feel the cold stone beneath it. It was difficult to breathe. He tried rolling over, using the bed to push against. Eventually he managed to shift his vast bulk over to one side. Lying on his side was painful as well.

*Cursed servants,* he thought. *They will all be punished.*

He struggled to lift himself to a sitting position. It was then that he smelled smoke. The fortress was burning! Fear struck his heart, not for himself (for the Khan was invulnerable), nor his servants (they were expendable), but for his treasure. In contrast to his servants, the accumulated fortune of a lifetime could not be replaced. With superhuman effort he hoisted himself to his feet. Then he accomplished a miracle. He walked.

With the kind of strength that only extreme panic produces, the Khan moved his immense body to the door and opened it. The hallway was steeped in darkness. But the route to his treasure chamber was etched so deeply in his mind, he needed neither light nor landmark to find his way. He advanced with heavy, determined steps until he reached the entrance to a small courtyard from which rose the central tower—the tower that none of his men had been able to find access to. The mystery of the tower's interior had never generated any interest in the Khan, for he would never be able to scale its heights. For him, the most attractive feature of the tower was the enormous cavern that lay at its base, under the courtyard. It had been hollowed out from the living rock that supported the weight of the castle and had but a single entrance: a locked metal door that only the Khan was allowed to open. The door opened onto a wide stairway that led directly down into the cavern. This huge, impenetrable vault had served as the Khan's safe for many years. The wealth it contained was unimaginable.

The Khan approached the courtyard, quaking with anxiety. He had no idea how he was going to remove his treasure. He only knew that he must guard it against harm. It was by sheer luck that the Khan arrived at his destination unscathed. Immense stones, dislodged by the force of the thunderbolt that had jolted the Khan from his bed, fell to earth, the echoes of their descent resounding like small explosions in the enclosed space of the inner courtyard. Somehow he made his way to the door. He clutched at his chest, where the key to his treasure chamber lay snug, next to his heart. Blindly, he inserted it into the lock and pushed until the heavy brass door swung open.

Even in the blackness of the unlit grotto, the treasure of the Khan shone, seemingly with a light of its own. He sighed. This was his dream, his life, his world. Gleaming precious metals, plates of copper, silver, and gold; gems of every shape, size, and color: amethysts, rubies, sapphires, diamonds, emeralds, and topaz; strings of pearls; droplets of amber and amulets of jade; diadems, circlets, and even crowns from the kings he had defeated—all lay piled in great, luminous mounds. He pushed the door shut behind him. With the Khan keeping watch, his treasure would be safe—for all time.

Six bodies lay on the wet stones. From above they looked like discarded toys, left out in the rain by some thoughtless child. A damsel with tangled hair had been thrown carelessly atop her knight. A king, along with his noble steed, had been tossed into a corner. A great snow crane, its white wings spread in an awkward fan, was stretched beside a small brown seal. They lay tumbled in little heaps, the forgotten playthings of the gods.

It was Gertrude who broke the silence. She rose on unsteady legs. The floor trembled beneath her hooves. She nuzzled Elissa uneasily.

"Get up!" she brayed.

There was no movement. Gertrude brayed louder.

The knight stirred. Something was weighing Favian down. He lifted an arm and brushed the hair from his face. Then he looked down at his chest, where Elissa's pale face was nestled amid a tangle of curls. Her body was slumped heavily against him. She was lying perfectly still, though Gertrude was making enough noise to wake the dead. Favian struggled to sit up.

"Elissa!" He shook the limp girl by her shoulders. "Wake up!" She lay unmoving under his hands. He held a strand of her hair beneath her nostrils. It didn't stir. All the while, Gertrude kept pushing her soft nose against Elissa's face and neck, huffing frantically. Finally the donkey looked entreatingly into Favian's face, the tears of a woman in grief rolling freely from her soft brown eyes.

A deep, wrenching sob tore its way out of Favian's chest. He clutched the lifeless girl, unconscious of the incoherent sounds he was making, numb to every thought but the one that was now destroying him.

"Oh, Elissa," he moaned. She had lain with him in death as she never would in life; had spread her soft hair over his face, placed her cheek upon his chest, and closed her eyes forever. He stroked her damp hair, his fingers still tingling from the bolt that had coursed through his body. In his heart were all the things he had never told her, had never had the courage to tell her. And now it was too late. Heart pressed to heart, he held Elissa against his chest, wrapping his arms around her still body. Then he felt it—a tiny stirring from deep within her. Life! Without thinking, Favian placed both hands upon her chest and willed the lightning to come again—this time not from the sky, but from his body. Favian had no idea what the consequences of such an action might be, but now was not the time for self-doubt.

Elissa's chest jerked once, twice; then, with a deep, rasping sob, she took in a great gulp of air. The color returned to her face. She opened her eyes. Favian blinked rapidly, momentarily speechless with relief and joy.

"Are you all right?" he said finally.

Elissa nodded. Favian helped her rise to her feet, and, steadying her against his side, he looked around for the others. Aesha and Maya were attempting to stand, leaning on one another for support against the continual shuddering of the tower. In the far corner of the room, Falk had half risen. He looked dazed. Favian took Elissa by the hand and, with the aid of Gertrude, they made their way to Falk. Aesha and Maya followed.

"We have to get out of here. The tower is collapsing," Favian said, leaning over to help Falk to his feet. Falk's eyes were open but unfocused, as if he were looking at something in the far distance. If he heard Favian, he showed no sign.

"We have to go," Favian repeated. "Right

now." He took Falk by one arm. Elissa held the other.

"There is only one way out," said Favian, pointing to the stairs.

As if in validation, the floor tilted crazily, dumping all of them into the stairwell.

If the journey to the top of the tower had seemed interminable, the journey down the spiral staircase was all too brief. They found themselves flung from stair to stair, cascading down whole flights at a time. Elissa desperately tried to keep her balance, but as the tower shifted and shook, they tumbled into one another, like dice rattling in a tall cup. All at once the stairway disappeared, and for one truly mad moment Elissa believed that they had landed safely at the bottom. However, it was not the bottom of the tower that opened up beneath them, but the side. A great chunk of stone the size of a small house had fallen out. The entire top of the tower had toppled over and was spinning crazily in the air, shaking out the little dice as it crashed downward to the earth. Elissa, flying through the starlit air for the second and last time, could not help but marvel at the view. She could see everything. The boats in which they had arrived tilted and swayed in the harbor, their anchors straining against the rising sea. From this height they looked like a child's toys. Falling took forever. As she fell, Elissa not only had time to observe the harbor, she could see that the rest of the castle was collapsing as well. All around her, the wind shrieked and howled.

Elissa waited for the ground to meet her in its final crushing embrace. She closed her eyes.

When her body finally encountered something solid, it was not with a crash, as she had expected, but with a whoosh. Suddenly she was no longer falling. Neither was she smashed to bits. Instead, she found herself encased in a huge set of claws that bore her safely to earth. The Phoenix opened her talons and, dropping Elissa, rose quickly to snatch Favian, Aesha, Maya, Gertrude, and Falk in mid-air. As the last of them was plopped unceremoniously on the ground, Elissa could have sworn she saw the Bird wink. Then, as abruptly as the Phoenix had appeared, she was gone—this time, Elissa suspected, for good.

The Phoenix had deposited them at a safe

distance from the tower. The monolith was fast losing its height. Even as they watched, mesmerized, it seemed to collapse in upon itself. The smaller parapets that had surrounded the inner courtyard slowly crumbled, one by one. Yet the rumbling and swaying beneath their feet indicated that they were not out of danger.

Favian shouted to make himself heard above the crashing of the towers. "I think the island may be sinking!" he cried. There was only one avenue of escape, and Favian knew exactly where to find it. He led them seaward.

As they headed toward the cliffs, Favian wondered if they would make it. From the increasing shudders of the ground beneath their feet, he calculated that they wouldn't have much time before the entire island broke apart. Even from this distance he could hear the breakers as they cast themselves furiously against the cliffs. On his downward flight from the tower, he had noted that the sea had risen considerably since they had arrived. Favian didn't like to think of the implications, but only hoped that one of the ships was still afloat.

Maya and Aesha flanked Favian, matching

his stride. Elissa led Gertrude, who kept up a steady trot in spite of the shifting of the earth. Soon they came to the edge of the cliffs. The stairway they had climbed only the day before had been engulfed. It was hard to imagine, but in the past few hours, the sea had risen nearly to the top of the cliff. Favian looked across to the harbor. Even if one of the ships had weathered the storm, there would be no way to reach it. To attempt to swim across this angry sea would be foolish—fatal. He looked back at the group, seeking direction, a second opinion.

Someone was missing.

"Where is Falk?" shouted Favian.

Elissa looked at him in horror. "I thought he was with you!" she cried.

Before Favian could reply, Elissa had turned around and begun to head back toward the still-crumbling castle. He reached out to grab her arm.

"Let go," said Elissa, her pale face determined. "I'm going back for him."

"No, you are not. Stay here with the others until I return."

"But," said Elissa, "he may be lost . . ." She didn't want to finish her thought: *Or buried alive.*

Favian looked into her pleading eyes, and very briefly pressed his hands against her shoulders, willing her to stay. Then, without wasting another word, Favian sprinted back along the path they had just taken.

Favian ran, the wind at his back. All at once, the ground stopped shaking, becoming firm and steady once again. He was grateful for the sudden calm, yet apprehensive. The stillness had an ominous feel to it, as though the earth were preparing itself for a final great heave. The darkness pressed in on him. Dawn must surely be about to break by now. It seemed to be taking forever in this corner of the world. Perhaps the sun would never rise again. It was possible. After this night, Favian could believe anything.

He ran on and on—through the smoking ruins of the fortress walls; over piles of stone, shattered beams, and lintels—his thoughts disjointed. The lightning, the Phoenix, the Khan, Falk—all tumbled together as in a kaleidoscope of images. Still Favian ran steadily, his exhaustion numbing him to his own effort. He was just getting to the point of forgetting why he was running at all when he stumbled and fell. A body lay in his path. He turned it over, prepared for the worst. It was not Falk, or anyone else he recognized. The body wore neither armor nor weaponry, so it was probably one of the servants. He must be near the living quarters of the castle, then. Heedless of who might hear him, Favian shouted. In the chaos of the castle's fall, it was unlikely the Khan's guard would have been able to organize an attack against him, even if they had survived.

"Falk!" Favian's cry sounded shrill, panicky, to his own ears. Other than the crunching of settling rubble and the popping of flames, there was no answering sound. He called again. This time he heard a response, a name. But it was not Favian's name that echoed among the stones.

Favian headed toward the origin of the cry. In what had once been the inner courtyard surrounding the central tower, he found Falk wandering aimlessly among the fallen walls. The man halted and turned upon Favian's approach, though he did not seem to recognize him.

"Galantha, my wife. I cannot find her." Falk was weeping openly.

Favian held out his hand, offering it to the distraught king. Although he did not know where Galantha was, he was sure she would not make another appearance in this world. "Come along," he said softly. "She is not here."

Falk did not move. A tremor shook the ground. As Favian had suspected, their reprieve was going to be a short one.

"Come with me." Favian tried to speak gently, persuasively, in spite of the urgency of their situation. "Elissa is expecting you."

"Elissa . . . where is she?" Falk looked as if he was trying to focus.

Favian waved toward the edge of the cliffs. "She is waiting for us . . . with the others. Come, now. We have to join her."

A dark figure emerged from the shadows, his sword drawn and his lips spread in an all-too-familiar leer. "Indeed we do!"

"There is no justice," muttered Favian as he drew his sword. "Why you?" he said. "Anybody with any sense would be dead by now."

"As you will soon be," rasped Kreel. He circled

around them, a knife in one hand and a sword in the other. "Your King is befuddled," he observed. "And unarmed." He made a quick lunge toward Falk, trying to open up Favian's defense.

Favian, however, was impervious to feints. He was fed up with Kreel, disgusted with the perverted Khan, and he'd been pushed to the point of total pinpoint concentration. All he wanted right now was to skewer Kreel's heart on the end of his sword. And nothing was going to stop him from attaining that goal.

Favian thrust his sword toward Kreel. Caught off guard, Kreel leapt back, though he soon regained his balance. Kreel was quick. Unlike Favian, Kreel had not missed an entire night of sleep. Nor had he been tortured, hit by lightning, and flung from the tallest tower in the world. Kreel managed a parry and, maintaining a firm stance, executed a series of quick, vicious attacks.

Favian countered each thrust as it came, his expression grim. Kreel was trying to back him into a corner, and Favian knew it. He feinted and reeled to the side. Kreel pursued him, the scars on his face livid.

"Let me tell you what I'm going to do," whispered Kreel. "I'm going to carve up that little hussy of yours, exactly like I was."

In a fury, Favian attacked, driving Kreel back. He could not speak; he needed all his breath. But his mind blazed. And Kreel defended himself, doggedly, gradually turning his defense into an attack, thrusting at Favian's face, neck, chest.

"But first I am going to dispose of her doddering father and obnoxious boyfriend." Kreel pressed on, forcing Favian to retreat. A fine line of spittle edged Kreel's lips, making him look like the rabid dog he was.

Favian fought valiantly. With each thrust he parried; with each lunge he dipped, spun, and countered. The exchanges were swift, as neither man wore armor or carried a shield. Favian was the better of the two swordsmen, but the night had taken its toll on him. As he searched for higher ground, he thought of the number of times he had escaped disaster that night. He clamped his teeth together. Blast all the gods if Kreel would be the one to send him into the Underworld! Yet he could feel his defense weakening by the moment.

"And when you're dead, she'll be mine," Kreel

rasped. His lips were spread wide, triumphant. "Say your prayers, boy."

Favian didn't know any prayers. It was his mother, the Countess Rowenna, who had sung to the gods, appeased them, placated them. It was she who had taught him to control his power over fire. But he had nothing to say to the gods, for they had abandoned him to his fate. There wasn't a spark of energy left in him; all of it had been used on the Phoenix. The only thing left to him now was sheer will—and discipline. He focused his remaining strength not on his arms holding the sword, nor on his legs seeking safe purchase on the uneven ground, but on his palms. And he thought of the woman who had taught him so well.

*Mother*, he prayed. There came a familiar tingling. It passed from his palms to his fingers, then flowed into the sword. Briefly, the blade glowed, the metallic edge turning ruddy before bursting into flame.

Astonished, Kreel paused in mid-strike, and in that fatal moment of disorientation he dropped his guard. Favian took in Kreel's distorted face— the points of his few yellowed teeth emerging from his slack mouth, his malevolent sunken eye. And Favian knew beyond a shadow of a doubt that his sword was about to separate that hideous head from its body. Screaming in defiance, Favian rushed in for one last violent attack. He swept his fiery blade in an arc, splitting Kreel's sword in two, and then, aiming at Kreel's neck for the final killing blow, he leapt.

But the blow never came. The earth, in a single mighty heave, had flicked Favian back as easily and lightly as a dog shakes off an irritating flea. As Favian landed, the ground, with a wrenching shudder, began to ripple. Belying its nature, the earth flowed like water, making it impossible to stand. Favian lay flat, gripping the surface with his hands, while, heaving and groaning, the earth split itself in two. When the great tearing finally stopped and the earth merely shivered, like a small, injured animal, Favian lifted his head. The ground Favian had been standing on had vanished, leaving in its place a gaping chasm. In spite of the danger, Favian crawled forward and peered over the side of the rift. He was stupefied by what he saw.

*So the myth is true,* he thought. *The center of the*

*earth* is *lined with gold.* For all the riches of the earth lay within the abyss—precious stones, gleaming; coveted metals; crystals; sparkling gems. And bags—piles and piles of brown burlap sacks, hundreds of them lay amongst the treasure.

Favian shifted himself to his knees and searched for his sword. There was still a battle to be fought, though with luck, Kreel had been buried in that last quake. Favian lifted his head. Too late he realized his error, for directly across from him, at the edge of the earth's open wound, Kreel was poised, his knife balanced in his hand, ready to be thrown. Favian tried to hurl himself out of its path.

But just as Favian's sword had not fallen on Kreel, the knife never found Favian's flesh. Focused on the target of his wrath, Kreel had not noticed Falk creeping up behind him. He felt the push that sealed his fate a second too late. As Kreel tumbled—down, down, into the chasm— he saw emerging from the glittering treasure two enormous arms, reaching up to receive him. Then, with a deep, low groan, the fissure closed in upon itself with a thud. It was all over in an instant.

"I'm ready to go now," said Falk. He was wiping his hands on the front of his tunic, as though he had touched something slimy.

Favian stood and located his sword. The ground had started to shiver again.

"Let's go, then," said Favian. As he walked forward, a thin line of flames appeared at his feet. Small fires seemed to be springing up everywhere, as if from the earth itself.

The true peril of their situation suddenly revealed itself to Favian. He turned to Falk, who was picking his way cautiously through the rubble. "We have to hurry, my lord. Those sacks. When the flames reach them, they'll ignite."

They ran through the ruins, the heaving of the earth making every step an effort. All around them, small stones fell in a sharp, insistent hail. And to make matters worse, a pre-dawn sea fog had begun to settle. It drifted over the shifting stones, making each step a potential disaster. After what seemed like an eternity, Favian and Falk returned to the harbor. As the two men emerged stumbling from the mist, their arms supporting each other, Elissa let out a cry of joy.

"They're back!" she shouted. She ran forward

to embrace them both. Her father looked as if he'd somehow aged and Favian seemed about to drop from exhaustion, but they were alive!

"Elissa," said Favian. "We have to get off the island right now."

"Maya has found us a launch," said Elissa. The little girl was standing thigh-deep in the water, steadying the side of the boat so they could all climb aboard. As he let go of Falk's arm, the earth convulsed and Favian lost his footing and fell, but he rose again as a small wave washed against him. Elissa took his arm and helped him aboard.

They huddled inside a medium-sized launch, which, miraculously, had not lost its oars. It looked large enough to accommodate them all. Gertrude had already taken her place in the stern. She looked profoundly unhappy. The boat creaked and protested, and settled deeply into the water. Finally Maya gave the launch a push and jumped in herself.

"There had better be a ship out there," mumbled Favian. "I can't swim."

Elissa didn't reply. Even if Favian could swim,

it would be pointless. There was no place to go. Aesha and Maya rowed steadily away from the island. The sea was still rough, but the waves had lost their fury, having little to hurl themselves against. Aesha hummed soothingly as she rowed, the dying wind responding to her melody with its departure. As they drew farther from the island, Elissa looked back on their progress.

From this distance, the island looked like a small hill rising straight out of the sea. The sun was about to rise, and in the early dawn the island appeared ghostlike. Suddenly the sun burst upon the earth.

The explosion was deafening.

Elissa held her ears and screamed.

Moments later the sky began to rain small pieces of stone and bits of dirt. Elissa and the others cradled their heads in their arms, protecting themselves against the barrage.

Which is why nobody saw the wave.

Twenty feet high and as long as the island was wide, it struck the boat broadside. As they rode up its enormous flank, the crest broke over the side of the launch. They bailed furiously with their hands, but it was useless. There was too much weight in the boat. The floorboards were beginning to separate beneath their feet. Gertrude began to bray pathetically.

The small party seemed to come to the realization that their situation was hopeless all at the same time. Favian and Falk; Maya, Aesha, and Elissa—all stopped bailing. They looked at one another—a small brown child; a tall, pale woman with a little bird on her shoulder; a tired youth in need of a shave; a man with graying hair and mournful eyes; and a young, green-eyed girl on the cusp of life. All at once, Maya stood up and dove overboard. A moment later, they felt the boat lift slightly; then it wobbled and sank down into the water again.

Maya's head bobbed in the water beside the boat.

"It's too heavy," she said, her face infinitely sad. "I can't keep it afloat."

Elissa looked into Maya's brown eyes. "I'm sorry I never got you home to your mother," she said softly.

"I am home," replied Maya. "This is my Mother. I thought you already knew that."

"Perhaps I did," said Elissa.

As the sun cast its first rays upon the sinking launch, Maya reached her arms up for a final goodbye.

"I can't save you," the girl sobbed.

Elissa patted the girl's dripping hair. "You can save Sweetheart," she said. Elissa told the little bird to go, and it fluttered from Aesha's shoulders, circling her head twice before settling on Maya's head.

"My love," it warbled plaintively. Aesha looked at Maya, seeming to truly see her for the first time.

"Take him back to Billy for me," said Aesha. The little girl nodded her head, salt tears streaming from her eyes into the salty sea.

Falk was gazing at his daughter as she said her goodbyes. His heart still ached for the apparition that had once again been his, all too briefly. But there was no holding on to the past, nor, it seemed, to the future. There was something he had wanted to tell Elissa when they returned to Castlemar, something he had wanted to say for a long time. He looked into Elissa's green eyes, perhaps for the last time, drinking them in.

"I love you," he said simply.

Elissa felt her heart swell, and in that moment, it did not matter at all if these were the last words she would hear on earth, for they were the best.

"I know," she said. "But it's good to hear you say it."

"Uh," said Favian. "I am sorry to interrupt, but there is a matter of, uh, some importance, at least to me . . ."

"Just spit it out, man!" yelled Gertrude. "Can't you see we're up to our withers in brine?"

"What did she say?" asked Favian suspiciously. "Is she talking about me?"

" 'Just spit it out, man!' " Elissa translated faithfully.

"What?" said Favian, taken aback. But if she wanted him to "spit it out," he would. He spoke tentatively. "Well, I was just wondering . . . uh . . . if you wouldn't mind considering me as a suitor."

"*Now* you ask?" Elissa stared at Favian in disbelief. The boat was sinking fast. Little waves were breaking over the sides.

"Well, I might not have another opportunity,"

replied Favian defensively. "I know my timing is a little off."

"Yes," said Elissa.

"Yes, I don't have the best timing? Or yes, you wouldn't mind having me for a suitor?" Favian was trying to hold his sword up out of the water as he spoke. A true warrior would never allow his weapon to rust.

"Both!" cried Elissa.

Favian grinned. He would have hugged her, if not for the sword. And the waves.

"Good choice." Falk nodded approvingly.

Gertrude began to thrash as the launch sank beneath them. Elissa put a comforting arm around her. The frightened donkey wouldn't last long in the open sea. She was braying furiously.

"Stop strangling me!" yelled Gertrude. "I'd rather die just once, if you don't mind!"

Elissa, who normally paid scant attention to Gertrude's grumbling, didn't even hear her this time. She was focused on another sound—a great protesting groan that could not have originated from the sea or from any of its creatures. Within moments an ungainly craft hove into view, bearing down hard upon them. As it approached, the boat revealed itself to be an outlandish, rambling contraption upon which the full sails of an oceangoing vessel had been grafted.

"Gertie! Gertie, darling! Do not fear, Ralphie is here!"

A moment later, strong hands reached down into the churning waters. First Gertrude, the most difficult to lift, was hauled on board, to be reunited with an ecstatic camel, who nuzzled the donkey all over.

"Slobber away!" she cried. "I can't get any wetter!"

Shortly thereafter, the rest of them were plucked from the sea. Almost before they could comprehend what was happening, they had been laid side by side on the deck, like sardines in a tin. Even Maya came aboard. A stocky bearded man walked up and down the deck, piling blankets upon them all. Elissa sat up, completely dumbfounded.

"Cappy! How on earth did you find us? I thought you hated the sea."

The Captain lifted his cap to scratch his head. "It was Billy; he led us to yer. And that tea ye gave Doc works like a charm. Never felt better!" The Captain slapped Billy on the back as the boy passed by with a bale of hay for Gertrude. "Right fine navigator, Bucko, me boy," he chuckled.

Billy's freckled face broke into a broad, lopsided grin. "Nothing to it, miss," he said humbly. "I just followed the wee fishies and birdies."

The Captain winked at Elissa. "All he needed was a good reason to come all the way out here." He nodded in Aesha's direction. "And there she be! Yer tea will be coming soon."

"Is Doc on board, too?"

"No, he's portside, with me mum," explained Billy. "Doc's sort of in love, I guess." Billy was wrapping Aesha in a blanket as he spoke. He glanced briefly at Elissa and blushed scarlet before turning back to adjust the cloth tenderly around the Windsinger. Billy could hardly tear his eyes from her beautiful pale face. He could look at her forever. In fact, he intended to. Aesha gazed back at him, her eyes clear and bright, full of dawn.

A tiny woman approached them, balancing a tray loaded with cups of steaming tea in her arms.

"Om Chai! What on earth are you doing here?" Elissa sputtered. It was all too much.

The Captain jerked a thumb at Om Chai. "The old dame here said she needed a lift to Castlemar. So we gave her one, seeing as Billy wanted to come up that way. When we arrived, they said the king, yer *dad*, had gone off to fetch yer." The Captain squinted. "Tried to pull a fast one on me, didn't yer?"

Elissa nodded dumbly. "And Ralph?"

"Who's Ralph?" The Captain looked around the deck, as if trying to locate a hidden member of the crew.

"The camel," explained Elissa.

The Captain scratched his head. "Well, that is a puzzle," he said. "But I learned a long time ago not to ask questions where deliveries are concerned." The Captain wandered away, still scratching his head.

"Tea?" Om Chai held out a cup to Elissa, cocking her head in her peculiar birdlike manner.

"Thank you." Elissa felt a bit dazed.

As Elissa took the cup, Om Chai pointed with her chin toward the island. Elissa looked back, over her shoulder. All that was visible was a jagged piece of rock standing straight up from the sea. The tip of the tower. For a moment it blazed golden with the first rays of the sun. Then, with a sound like a deep sigh, it was suddenly gone, swallowed by the sea in one smooth gulp. A swirl of water, and World's End was no more.

Elissa turned back and took the tea. "The end of the world?"

"The beginning . . ." Om Chai smiled enigmatically, as is the way of prophets, and proceeded down the deck with her tray of cups.

Elissa closed her eyes and lay back. She could not imagine things could get any stranger. She felt someone stir beside her and cracked one eye open.

"What you said in the boat?" asked Favian cautiously. "You haven't reconsidered, have you?"

Elissa propped herself up on one elbow and laughed.

"No, I haven't had enough time to consider, let alone *re*consider," she said. But then, as Favian looked crushed, she relented. "The answer is still yes, Favian; just don't rush me."

"Oh, I won't," said Favian earnestly. "I don't think anybody *could.*"

Elissa sat up. She smiled as she took Favian by one hand and Falk by the other. She had no doubt that, with time, the two men in her life would learn to live with one another—and with her. Then she lifted her face to the sun, which rose majestically, generously endowing the new day, the new earth, with its radiance, reminding her of the warmth of her mother's sweet smile, freely given with all her heart. A single star twinkled on the horizon, like an old, forgotten wish that has just been granted.

"Let's go home," she said. "To Castlemar."

The star winked once and disappeared.

# Epilogue

Perhaps you have heard other tales recounting the adventures of Elissa, and of how she left her tranquil valley to travel far and wide with her faithful companions Maya the Water Girl, Aesha the Windsinger, Count Favian the Firemaker, and Gertrude the donkey. Maybe you already know the story of how the evil Khan was vanquished by his own unmitigated greed. You may even have heard the legend of the Phoenix, and of how Elissa saved the world. There are many such stories told around a crackling fire on a cold winter's night. But what you have not yet heard is the end of this tale.

Elissa returned with her companions to Castlemar, though Aesha and Maya were not to remain there long. Aesha, her voice restored, decided to return to the sea—with Billy Buck, the finest navigator in the world. Unlike any other navigator, Billy could accurately locate his ship's position without the aid of a compass, sextant, or star, solely by the movements of the sea and her creatures. It seemed he had a Gift. The exploits of the famous seaman and his singing consort are known the world over. But even though they sailed the length and breadth of the widest seas, reaching the most far-flung of the earth's exotic lands, they always found time to berth in Castlemar.

Maya went back to her island home, only to discover that her mer-family had abandoned the land and returned to their Mother, the sea. Not one to be left out, Maya decided to join them, and they, of course, received her joyfully. Having the full run of the sea, she swam up to visit Elissa regularly. To this day she can be seen sunning her sleek brown body on the rocks along Castlemar's shore.

Favian returned to Leonne, but only briefly. As with so many long-sought prizes, he soon tired of its achievement—as well as his perpetually

bickering courtiers. After spending many fruitless months enmeshed in bitter squabbles over
elaborate points of honor, mediating endless
property disputes over tiny bits of dry land, and
foiling one assassination plot after another, he
abdicated, leaving Leonne in the surprisingly
competent hands of his uncle Theo. Having
learned a valuable lesson from Sonia's rise and
fall, Theo dispensed wisdom and justice regard-
less of his, or anyone else's, personal interests.

Although Castlemar was her official home,
High Crossing was where Elissa could be found
in the milder months, accompanied, of course, by
Favian. When he finally abandoned Leonne, Favian had been eager to take her to the North
Country, though he had not initially understood
why she laughed so much at her first sight of Favian's "secret valley." Much to Bruno's delight, the
two of them made a habit of visiting every summer thereafter. It was during one of these summer sojourns that Favian and Elissa were joined
as husband and wife by Om Chai, with the assistance, of course, of their closest friends, human and nonhuman. (Although Favian declined

Ralph's generous offer to be best man, preferring to carry the ring himself.) In summer, when the wildflowers fill the high pastures with their sweet scent, and the waterfalls cast rainbows over Bruno's sparkling emerald valley, the red and white roses that bloom over the doorway of Favian and Elissa's stone cottage glow like fire, and the walls ring with the laughter of children.

Gertrude and Ralph continued to be steadfast companions. To make their union complete, they were married in a simple ceremony by Om Chai, who had accompanied them to Castlemar. For the great event, Gertrude wore a fragrant garland of waxy white Flowers of Lyss, and Ralph bore a stunning jewel-encrusted turban upon his head. The stable was packed with well-wishers of every species, bird and beast alike. Elissa acted as maid of honor, holding Gertrude's bouquet for her, as much to keep it out of reach of Gertrude's teeth as to maintain the appearance of proper wedding decorum. Favian was best man, and even he had to admit that the speeches were moving. After Om Chai had declared them mates for life, Ralph slobbered all over Gertrude and everyone cried— especially the chickens. Although, to Ralph's profound disappointment, they never had children, the two were happy, and remained inseparable for the rest of their lives.

Falk remained King until he was reunited with his beloved Galantha in the Spirit World, whereupon Elissa became Queen of Castlemar. Although she was Queen, for the most part her kingdom was managed by a consortium of silk producers, farmers, and seamen who, with Elissa's guidance, had organized themselves into a group of cooperatives. Much to the dismay of the nobility, she ran an entirely informal court, addressing the servants as equals and banishing high heels. When the nobles protested, Elissa simply did away with all tithes and taxes, which meant that when their money ran out, even the Cousins were forced to do something useful. And soon, either because their monarchs were weary of court intrigues or because their peasants had organized, the smaller kingdoms between Castlemar and Leonne followed suit, and within a generation there was peace, prosperity, and equity all over the world.

As for the Phoenix, it will be centuries before she once again takes human form. And many more years will pass before she sends her chosen one to seek out the Elements that will enable her to continue her perpetual cycle of decay and re-generation. Meanwhile, those who walk the bountiful green earth are advised to do so with care—because those who walk lightly upon the earth keep their balance.

# Acknowledgments

I would like to thank my editor, Heidi Kilgras, for her unflagging—and unflinching—energy in editing this trilogy, as well as for her keen editor's eye. Her stamina was nothing short of heroic; her faith, inspiring. Her assistant, Christy Webster, whose enthusiasm lent much life and vigor to the project, made numerous valuable contributions, all of which were appreciated. I would also like to thank Carolyn Jenks for representing the trilogy.

This series has enjoyed the benefit of input from many readers, stemming back from the time when it was but a short novella. Jane Johnson was the first to suggest that Elissa be portrayed as a "grrl," which was much more in keeping with her real-life model. Simms Buckley offered her generous support and encouragement, as did Anne Williams and Diana Tanaka from overseas. Later, my "guinea pigs," Kacie and Emily Eaton, contributed their comments, and gave invaluable feedback from the perspective of young "tweens." Their father, John Eaton, was a mainstay—photographer, webmaster, and all-around rock in a stormy sea. Special thanks go to Ruth Hairston and Francine Vidal, my two angels of mercy, and to Lauren Gellman, a true friend.

Even before Elissa was a glimmer in her author's eye, my two children, Maya and Tim, had already made her real. Many years before Maya insisted that I put the stories into print, Elissa was an integral part of our nightly bedtime routine. Her escapades never ceased to delight them, and my children never ceased to inspire me. They continue to do so. And so this, as with all my endeavors, must ultimately be laid at their door. My greatest pleasure will be to see what wonders they have in store for us.

Erica Verrillo is a world traveler who has studied and worked in a variety of fields, including classical music, Latin American history, linguistics, folk dance, anthropology, refugee aid, and speech communication. She has been a teacher of foreign languages, ESL, public speaking, linguistics, and music. She lives in Syracuse, New York.